EDWIN A. ABBOTT (1838–1926), a Victorian of great intellect and wit, enjoyed success not only as a writer, but as a scholar, educator, and theologian. Educated at St. John's College, Cambridge, he was Headmaster of the City of London School from 1865 to 1889. During that time, his progressive belief in the importance of the study of English for every student, even before traditional classic curriculum, led him to write *A Shakespearian Grammar* (1870), "to help solve most of the difficulties that will present themselves to boys." It ran to three editions within its first year of publication alone and continues to be a touchstone for Shakespearian scholars. In 1884 he wrote *Flatland*. First considered by many as merely "a pleasant tonic, and an excellent stimulant for boys," it was later recognized as a magnificent work of science fiction, as prophetic as those of Jules Verne and H.G. Wells. Retiring to a scholarly life in 1889, he produced numerous other works, including *Silanus the Christian* (1907), *Apologia: an explanation and defense* (1907), *Message of the Son of Man* (1909), and *Light on the gospel from an ancient poet (Odes of Solomon)* (1913).

FLATLAND

A ROMANCE OF MANY DIMENSIONS

With Illustrations by the Author,
A SQUARE

EDWIN A. ABBOTT

With an Introduction by A.K. Dewdney

A SIGNET CLASSIC
NEW AMERICAN LIBRARY
NEW YORK AND SCARBOROUGH, ONTARIO

Introduction copyright © 1984 by NAL PENGUIN INC.

SIGNET, SIGNET CLASSIC, MENTOR, ONYX, PLUME, MERIDIAN
and NAL BOOKS are published *in the United States* by NAL PENGUIN INC.,
1633 Broadway, New York, New York 10019,
in Canada by The New American Library of Canada Limited,
81 Mack Avenue, Scarborough, Ontario M1L 1M8

First Signet Classic, Printing, June, 1984

3   4   5   6   7   8   9   10   11

PRINTED IN THE UNITED STATES OF AMERICA

To

The Inhabitants of SPACE IN GENERAL

And H. C. IN PARTICULAR

This Work is Dedicated

By a Humble Native of Flatland

In the Hope that

Even as he was Initiated into the Mysteries

Of THREE Dimensions

Having been previously conversant

With ONLY TWO

So the Citizens of that Celestial Region

May aspire yet higher and higher

To the Secrets of FOUR FIVE OR EVEN SIX Dimensions

Thereby contributing

To the Enlargement of THE IMAGINATION

And the possible Development

Of that most rare and excellent Gift of MODESTY

Among the Superior Races

Of SOLID HUMANITY

INTRODUCTION

The publication in England one hundred years ago of Edwin A. Abbott's *Flatland* was greeted by reviews which ranged from "fascinating" to "mortally tedious." On the one hand, Abbott (1838–1926) had described an amusing and curious two-dimensional world inhabited by flat creatures knowing no space higher than their own. On the other hand, Abbott made of the Flatlanders' ignorance a metaphor suggesting that we solid folk are no better off when it comes to higher realities. While many Victorian readers found Abbott's tabletop world fascinating and, of itself, reason enough for a book, others found Abbott's continuing insistence on the metaphor somewhat distracting. His approach appeared too didactic. Besides, what gave his "gospel of three dimensions" such urgency as to dominate the story?

One answer to this question emerges from a simple review of Abbott's life and work, his concern with religion generally and the Church of England in particular. Such concerns explain not only the urgency of Abbott's message but the form and content of his flat world and the flat society inhabiting it. Viewed closely through the lens of Abbott's satire, the Flatlanders invite our amusement with their pettiness and ignorance. Viewed from a higher vantage point, however, the satirical possibilities shrink in face of the challenge of the third dimension. Satire gives way to sobriety and we, like the Flatlanders, cringe before the possibilities of ascent. This ascent is really Abbott's cardinal point, and while we might imagine all sorts of physical or even theological significances for it, there can be little doubt that Abbott understood the ascent in a fairly specific way not revealed in his book.

Besides its length and breadth, Flatland (or perhaps we should say *Flatland*) has two other dimensions. The physical dimension embraces the world of Flatland and all of its inhabitants. The metaphysical dimension embraces the world "above" Flatland both in its implied relationship to the Flatlanders and in the symbolic content of that relationship for us. We will explore these additional dimensions before returning to Abbott's principal theme.

When we read about Flatland and witness a consistent two-dimensional world whose inhabitants live, move and perceive in harmony with two-dimensional laws, our fascination is really the surface manifestation of a deeper question. Once we have grasped the idea that flat things, objects of infinitesimal thickness, may participate in a physics totally within the plane and quite independent of our own, there is a dawning sense of mystery and wonder. How very odd! Could such a place really exist? This question is at once a philosophic and scientific one and it leads immediately to a host of related questions about our own universe. First, why does our universe have three physical dimensions and not two or four? Second, in what way does the three-dimensionality of our universe affect its physical, chemical, and biological processes? Once this box is opened it becomes very hard to close.

Given a degree of scientific credibility for a two-dimensional universe, we are inclined all the more readily to suspend disbelief in Flatland and its inhabitants. Although something tells us that it is ridiculous to suppose that "real" Flatlanders might be shaped like triangles and other geometrical figures, we accept the geometry as if the figures of Euclid had been given a life of their own and freedom to roam an infinite plane. The visual and tactile experiences of the Flatlanders harmonize with their two-dimensional environment in ways which the reader may easily confirm: for example, a Flatlander's entire visual world is contained within a single line subdivided into the objects of his perception.

The physical dimension of *Flatland* is complemented and, to a degree, even superseded by a metaphysical dimension, the one on which Abbott insisted so strongly. The hero of Flatland is a figure of geometric shape named A. Square—because he is one. Mr. Square is a young and idealistic flatlander who is visited one evening by a sphere from "Spaceland", the realm of three dimensions. In Flatland, the social hierarchy of geometrical beings is arranged so that the many-sided figures rule over those with fewer sides. The most powerful beings in Flatland therefore belong to the priestly class whose members have so many sides that they cannot be distinguished from circles. Imagine Square's astonishment when he is visited by a creature of the highest perfection who materializes in the middle of his room, first as a small circle and then as one of steadily increasing size. This is the noble Lord Sphere manifesting himself in Flatland in the only way he knows—as a cross section. What Square thinks is the whole turns out to be merely a part. This and other insights come only later to Square as he undergoes the most difficult educational experience of his life, supplemented by a trip to spaceland itself by courtesy of Lord Sphere. Abbott's account of the visitation by the sphere produces reverberations in our cultural memory: we recall how sages and divines from all spiritual traditions—including Christianity—have reported encounters with angelic or "higher" beings which appeared out of nowhere. What can Abbott's image be but an expression of such an encounter with all of its theological implications intact? The geometry of the participants, Mr. Square and Lord Sphere, serves to neutralize the human content of the encounter and so to express the metaphor at a more subliminal level. We are not *forced* to view the contact as a religious experience but merely as the intersection of a sphere with a plane—witnessed by a square. But the vibration is there and is reinforced enough times in the course of *Flatland*'s telling to leave no doubt that the metaphysical dimension is Abbott's main interest. He is trying to tell us something about our human failure to grasp higher realities. But does he mean to tell us, in effect, that God inhabits a fourth dimension or does he mean only to suggest that spiritual realities are merely *like* a fourth dimension, everywhere accessible but nowhere visible? This and other questions can be given only partial answers by examining Abbott's other works, but the answers are interesting and go a long way toward suggesting the metaphysical dimension of Abbott's metaphor.

Edwin A. Abbott was born in 1838 in London, raised in a solid Anglican family, and finished his education at St. John's College in Cambridge, where he was elected a fellow at the age of twenty-three. After two years as Assistant Master of the King Edward School in Birmingham, he was appointed headmaster of the City of London School, a prestigious educational posting. Ten years later he was made

Hulsean Lecturer at Cambridge, a position which undoubtedly pleased him as it gave him the opportunity of working out the implications of his own brand of rational Christianity.

Abbott, who had taken a divinity degree at Cambridge, was a devout clergyman and staunch supporter of the established church, taking as his special role the defense of the church against all forms of irrationality and superstition. A great admirer of Sir Francis Bacon and the enquiring rational mind which he exemplified, Abbott sought a complete reconciliation and harmony between his scientific convictions and his religious faith. There are hints among his many religious writings that he saw himself in an almost prophetic role as an exemplar of a new faith which had no dependence on "credulity." In the midst of a controversy arising from a book in which he criticizes Cardinal Newman's doctrine, Abbott declares:

> And when a man feels (as I do) that he has at last attained a profound spiritual truth which will, in all probability, be generally accepted by educated Christians who are not Roman Catholics, before the twentieth century is far advanced, he can well afford to be patient of prejudice.

One of the most important events in Abbott's life and, indeed one of the most important in nineteenth-century England, was the Tractarian controversy. The man at its center was an Anglican priest by the name of John Henry Newman. Vicar of St. Mary's, the University Church in Oxford, Newman published a document called *Tract 90* in 1841, a plea that the Church of England return to more traditional doctrines and practices. The tract created tremendous tension and dissension in the Church and, unable to persuade the Church of his views, Newman became a Roman Catholic in 1845, was ordained in Rome a year later and, ultimately, was made a cardinal by Pope Leo XIII. Newman was a man of tremendous magnetism and his conversion was seen as a direct threat to the established Church. Abbott was among those who could not accept Newman's arguments for change and regarded him as a man who had unconsciously duped himself and would dupe others. Specifically, Newman was prone to "credulity", an unscientific acceptance of unprovable and unlikely things. Although we do not find Newman in Flatland we find everywhere Abbott's stress on logical ability and personal experience as the basis of all knowledge, whether secular or religious.

Abbott was a busy and prolific writer of books, attested to by a bibliography which includes twenty religious works, eleven books of instruction, two biographies, and, of course, Flatland. The religious books range from children's stories of the New Testament to treatises on Biblical criticism. The instructional texts deal largely with English grammar, vocabulary, and good writing. The biographies concentrate on two men, the one Abbott most admired and the one he most despised—Bacon and Newman, respectively. In this literary landscape, Flatland stands out as a promontory, so to speak, a strange headland with seemingly little relation to its surroundings. Why should Abbott, this most rational of churchmen and proponent of sober, inquiring faith suddenly burst forth into imaginative flower with a work having no precedent and no successor among his books? What is Flatland trying to tell us which the other books cannot?

On closer inspection, Flatland seems a more logical part of Abott's literary output, at least when we reexamine the central concern of his life. Two especially important books provide a clue, *Philomythus: An Antidote Against Credulity* and *The Kernel and the Husk: Letters on Spiritual Christianity*. In these books Abbott tells us what must be taken on faith and what must be explained in Christianity. Again and again he attacks miracles as illusions or false reports and attempts to replace a belief in miracles by a faith in the "supernatural," a second category which to most readers appears hardly distinct from the first. Yet for Abbott the Supernatural means that which is both "obvious" and "obviously above "nature." The universe, he says, either had a beginning or it did not. Either possibility points to a phenomenon outside the scope of nature itself.

How can it not have bothered Abbott that he himself was incapable of explaining "supernature"? Could he really be so sure of a distinct boundary between it and the miraculous? He felt that the Supernatural might from time to time intervene in the natural world which humans inhabit but to do so it could in no way violate natural laws. This was the kernel of Abbott's belief and it needed support. At the same time such support could hardly come from a seemingly self-contained natural world (of any dimension) or from natural laws. Nor could it come from any logical argument based on the world or its laws. *Flatland* may well be Abbott's attempt to make the Supernatural credible (if not exactly explainable in any strict sense) as a kind of higher-dimensional influence. If a three-dimensional being could visit Mr. Square, so could a Higher Being have created *Flatland* (and, by implication, our own universe) in the first place. In fact, such a Being is explicitly mentioned in *Flatland* when Square holds converse with that ungraspable paragon of three-dimensional perfection, Lord Sphere:

> My Lord, your own wisdom has taught me to aspire to One even more great, more beautiful, and more closely approximate to Perfection than yourself. As you yourself, superior to all Flatland forms, combine many circles in One, so doubtless there is One above you who combines many Spheres in One Supreme Existence, surpassing even the Solids of Spaceland.

Flatland provides precisely the framework in which the Supernatural may comfortably exist in Abbott's mind. It implies a hierarchy of dimensions within which and upon which the Supernatural works its plan. If this is the case, how literally does Abbott wish us to take the metaphysical dimension of Flatland? The answer, in a nutshell, is simply "as literally as is necessary to combat credulity." Abbott would replace credulity with credibility.

Abbott is promoting a view of reality in which the natural and supernatural worlds exist together in the harmony of a multidimensional framework. All would seem logical, Abbott is telling us, if only we could *see*. Then tales of bleeding statues, miraculous cures, and other unlikely things would be understood for what they are—the chimeras and fantasies of unstable and credulous minds. Unfortunately, Abbott's multidimensional metaphysics allows for the very phenomena which he so despises: when a statue of the Virgin Mary cries, why could not her tears be introduced from a fourth dimension?

Apart from its physical and metaphysical dimensions, *Flatland* is a fascinating window on English Victorian culture. The most prominent features of Flatland society are its hierarchical structure and the role of women. In both cases geometry is the vehicle of Abbott's satire.

The class structure of Flatland is based almost entirely on how many sides one has. Triangles yearn to become squares while squares look up to pentagons and so on up to the "chief circle" who, in reality, is a polygon with several hundred sides. It would be extremely rude for a member of any class to misjudge the social rank of another by underestimating the number of his (dimly seen) sides, and so members of polite society cultivate the fine art of feeling each other's angles. One brief touch tells the informed practitioner of this subtle art the precise social standing of another. It may have delighted Abbott to mock the upper classes of nineteenth-century England by suggesting, in effect, that those of lower station grope about their figures to confirm their noble status. Undoubtedly, much of the amusement of Victorian readers sprang from the bizarre images suggested by a translation of Flatland social behavior directly into their own lives and times.

At the very lowest stratum of Abbott's two-dimensional society are the women, mere line segments, brainless beings given over entirely to the emotional side of life and incapable of the simplest logical deduction. A needle-shaped female represents the gravest possible threat to Flatland males through the possibility of piercing their sides by a careless movement of her posterior point. For this reason, the women are required to wiggle their posteriors back and forth so as to be periodically visible to all males in the vicinity. At the same time, they are required to utter little cries as a warning. Here is the clearest possible expression of stereotyped feminine Victorian behavior: the bustle, with its amplification of feminine anatomy, and the continual chatter, which Abbott implies is something to be avoided.

These examples suggest curious inversions in Abbott's way of looking at things: the substitution of touch for sight in the judging of one's fellows, as well as the interchanging of sexual roles in the act of "piercing" a member of the opposite sex. But more than this, the amusement occasioned by such imagery throws Flatland society and, by implication, Victorian society into critical relief. The residents of Flatland seem made almost pathetic by a kind of double satire in which their imprisonment in the plane only magnifies their foibles: being silly is one thing but being silly *and* the object of inspection by more highly placed beings—that is, the Victorian reader—is quite another. In this sense Abbott goes somewhat further than Pope, the eighteenth-century satirist whom he most admired. For if Pope would suggest that concern over a lock of hair is pointless, he offers no behavioral substitute beyond the implied "no". Abbott is suggesting that his own fellow creatures are not only given over to a trivial existence but that beings of a higher dimension are (or could be) aware of it all. In short, the details of Flatland society and the immersion of Flatlanders in all its petty peculiarities amounts to a vast web of distraction in which Flatlanders are caught and thereby fail to realize their own vertical possibilities.

The logic of Abbott's two-edged satire therefore demands an element of sobriety when Mr. Square reaches out to the third dimension. Flatland can only be funny if Spaceland is serious, and Victorians reading this book may have glanced nervously about their room once or twice when Lord Sphere visited Mr. Square. Abbott may not have participated in the attitudes toward the social hierarchy, toward women, and toward the other elements of Victorian society satirized by his book, but he undoubtedly counted the attitudes themselves as of little moment when placed beside the Higher Reality implied by his multidimensional framework. If silly, they were doubly silly, but even if absent, failure to appreciate this Reality was already a black mark against the uncaring denizens of Flatland.

Flatland begs some comparison with that other, better-known work of the Victorian imagination, *Alice in Wonderland*. Like Abbott, the author of the Alice books was a clergyman, Charles Lutwige Dodgson by name, better known as Lewis Carroll. While Abbott had received some mathematical training at Cambridge, Carroll was a professional mathematician. He taught mathematics at Oxford and even made a few minor contributions of his own in the field of logic. In Carroll the mathematical element predominated, in Abbott the spiritual.

The difference between the works reflects a difference between their authors. To put it somewhat crudely, Abbott's purpose was to instruct by amusement while Dodgson's was to amuse by instruction. Once Abbott had generated interest and excitement in his bizarre, two-dimensional microcosm, he made it the vehicle for his metaphysical message. Dodgson's characters, on the other hand, were continually instructing Alice, either like parents or like teachers. Doing so, they expounded seeming nonsense. Abbott's spiritual preoccupations forced him to be serious on at least one level while Dodgson's mathematical profession seemed to have driven him to relief in pure fantasy with no obvious message at all—except, possibly, the message that there is no message, that life is ultimately lived down a rabbit-hole or through a looking-glass.

At the same time, no single group has cherished, preserved and even used *Flatland* and the Alice books as much as the scientific community has. Both books have been used regularly over the years to illustrate points of physics, mathematics, astronomy, and so on. I can almost hear one of my own professors explaining relativistic motion:

A particle approaching the speed of light must expend ever-increasing amounts of energy for ever-decreasing gains in speed. The situation reminds one of the Red Queen in one of the Alice books. She says, "It takes all the running you can do to stay in the same place."

or the structure of our universe:

One way to visualize four-dimensional space-time is to think of a two-dimensional space with an added time dimension. Imagine Flatland and its creatures moving through a third, time dimension and tracing out world-lines as they go.

Like *Alice in Wonderland*, Flatland has inspired additional works, including *An Episode of Flatland*, published in 1907 by the American logician C.H. Hinton, *Sphereland*, published in 1965 by Dionys Berger, a Dutch physicist, and *The Planiverse* published in 1984 by A.K. Dewdney.

It is instructive to compare the two-dimensional worlds set forth in these books, especially the first two. As one becomes aware of alternative plane worlds, it becomes possible to ask "Which is more correct? What laws *ought* to hold in a two-dimensional universe and how would they influence its form and content? Would matter be possible and, if matter, would there (could there) be life?" An attempt to answer such questions can only be a project in scientific speculation since, obviously, no experiments can be performed. A speculator in two-dimensional science must make a few, simple assumptions and squeeze out of them the greatest number of interesting conclusions—an activity rather like mathematical research.

Abbott's world is seen as a flat, horizontal sheet within which his geometrical figures may glide in any of the compass directions. They know not of "up" or "down". Abbott's entire universe consist of this single, flat world. Mr. Square could presumably travel as far as he wished in any direction he chose. There is no gravity and there are no planets. To the uncritical eye such a world seems charmingly self-consistent and, therefore, believable. However, a closer examination of the Flatland environment reveals some bothersome defects: how do the Flatlanders move about within their realm? Even if Abbott had supplied them with limbs, it is not clear how they would propel themselves except by swimming through Flatland's air. How is Mr. Square's house anchored in place? In other words, while Flatland and everything in it are infinitesimally thin, zero-thickness in fact, it, in turn, must rest upon some kind of surface which acts as a support. Perhaps a kind of gravity causes Flatland to adhere to this surface and a kind of friction keeps houses in position. In any event, such an extradimensional prop would be a violation of the speculator's implicit rule that all phenomena in a two-dimensional universe shall be influenced, as far as possible, only by the laws of that universe, and no phenomenon may be explained by the intrusion or influence of phenomena adjacent to that universe.

Hinton's book, *An Episode of Flatland*, sketches a

rather different universe featuring a flat, two-dimensional planet called Astria. As the Earth is a ball, so Astria is a disc and the Astrians may walk upon its circular surface just as we Earthlings walk upon our spherical surface. In order to walk, Hinton's Astrians come equipped with two legs and, except for two arms and two eyes, they are otherwise just as geometrical as Abbott's creatures. Hinton's planet is a great improvement over Abbott's world in at least two respects. First it is the natural consequence of a few simple assumptions about a two-dimensional universe, namely that it has both matter and gravity. Second, the presence of a planetary surface provides a more physically reasonable stage upon which Hinton's tale may unfold. It seems a pity that, having gone to the trouble of setting up such a plausible world, Hinton should then condemn its charming inhabitants to a melodramatic plot involving the triumph of a socialistic revolt over totalitarian rule. Moreover, once he is fairly launched into his story, Hinton again and again ignores his physical premises with obvious blunders such as having a multitude of Astrians seated at a banquet table when it is not clear how more than two could dine at it—one at either end.

But Hinton, at least, had a clear grasp of a two-dimensional universe, for Astria circles a two-dimensional sun along with a companion planet called Ardaea. One can readily imagine other suns and other planets speckling the vast, two-dimensional sheet which is Hinton's universe. In fact, this very sheet may be curved into the form of a vast sphere and thereby form a model often used by cosmologists to explain the idea of an expanding universe. Almost twenty years after Hinton's book appeared, the astronomer Edwin Hubble discovered that our universe was organized into vast islands of stars—the galaxies—and that these islands were receding from each other at high speeds. The universe was expanding, but not in a way comprehensible to the man or woman in the street. For this reason, our three-dimensional universe was sometimes represented as the two-dimensional skin of a balloon speckled with galaxies: as the balloon was inflated the galaxies were all clearly seen to recede from each other, an image jocularly referred to by astronomers as "Hubble's Bubble."

The third book on two-dimensional worlds to appear was Dionys Berger's *Sphereland*, a novelistic exposition intended for the general reader interested in science. Berger uses the spherical universe we have just discussed to explain the curvature of space in our own universe as well as other physical and cosmological ideas. In this book residents of Flatland set out to discover whether their universe is curved by measuring the angles of an enormous triangle, two points of which can only be reached by spaceship. They find that the sum of these angles is greater than one hundred and eighty degrees, good evidence that the triangle lies within the surface of a sphere.

Berger allows for the possibility of space travel by giving Flatland the shape of a disc and then embedding it in his spherical universe. Flatlanders, in traveling to the edge of this disc, notice that the misty Flatland air becomes increasingly rarified and they may then see through it, out into the vastness of their plane universe, catching their first glimpse of stars, as it were. By this clever but somewhat tortuous device Berger is able to use the reader's familiarity with Flatland in order to extend Abbott's tale to an account of Mr. Square's grandson, a clever hexagon who takes part, ultimately, in the ambitious space curvature project.

Berger did not much advance the art of designing two-dimensional universes, beyond noticing that they could be curved and that their inhabitants would be able to measure such curvature directly. However, Berger did introduce a number of strange beasts into Flatland and displayed a primitive spaceship as well as a net for it to land in.

The fourth book on two-dimensional worlds, Dewdney's *The Planiverse*, describes how a class of computer science students accidentally contacts a two-dimensional world on their computer. The students had been developing a program to simulate events in a very simple two-dimensional universe of their own design, focusing on a planet they called "Astria" after Hinton's world. Suddenly one evening one of their simple, geometrical creatures began to say things outside the program's scope. It announced itself to belong to a world called "Arde," and soon thereafter the simple Astrian was transformed on the display screen into an outlandish creature of incredible complexity: the student simulation program had somehow fallen into lockstep with the real thing and the computer had been converted into a communication tool for exploring Arde and its inhabitants. Over the course of one summer the students followed the adventures of one "Yndrd" in his quest for the Beyond.

Arde is a direct extension of Hinton's planet, taking its name, in part, from Astria's sister-disc, Ardaea. It circles its own disc-shaped sun which, in turn, is one of the innumerable flat stars in one of the innumerable flat galaxies comprising the "Planiverse", Dewdney's name for his own, particular, plane-universe. The details of Arde and the Planiverse were worked out largely by Dewdney but not without some help from dozens of scientists and laypersons worldwide, who sent him everything from technical papers on two-dimensional atomic structure to designs for planar machines. These submissions were all in response to an article in the July, 1980 issue of *The Scientific American* in which Martin Gardner presented some of Dewdney's ideas regarding the possible existence of a two-dimensional universe.

The question of the existence of a two-dimensional universe, even in theory, embodies some very weighty philosophical and scientific issues. For example, is there some definite reason why our own universe has three physical dimensions? Roger Penrose, the English mathematical physicist, feels that this is an important question whose answer may well involve theorizing about the ultimate structure of space. In a more general vein it may be asked, "What is the relationship between the laws of our universe and the fact that it exists?" Does the universe give rise to its own laws or *vice versa*? Given its laws, does it exist because in some mathematical sense it *must*, or does it exist as the creation of some "outside" agency? This question was one that Einstein often pondered, and it becomes more immediate when we investigate the possibility of actually designing a universe different from our own. No matter how far we succeed in the attempt, how should we ever actually *construct* one? Such questions, one feels, bring us to the limit of what is humanly feasible and we turn to our own world once more with a strange, new respect for the mere fact that it exists!

And now to Flatland, that strange and charming nineteenth-century tabletop microcosm, source of speculation, and mirror of metaphysics.

A.K. Dewdney
University of Western Ontario

PREFACE TO THE SECOND
AND REVISED EDITION, 1884.
BY THE EDITOR

If my poor Flatland friend retained the vigour of mind which he enjoyed when he began to compose these Memoirs, I should not now need to represent him in this preface, in which he desires, firstly, to return his thanks to his readers and critics in Spaceland, whose appreciation has, with unexpected celerity, required a second edition of his work; secondly, to apologize for certain errors and misprints (for which, however, he is not entirely responsible); and, thirdly, to explain one or two misconceptions. But he is not the Square he once was. Years of imprisonment, and the still heavier burden of general incredulity and mockery, have combined with the natural decay of old age to erase from his mind many of the thoughts and notions, and much also of the terminology, which he acquired during his short stay in Spaceland. He has, therefore, requested me to reply in his behalf to two special objections, one of an intellectual, the other of a moral nature.

The first objection is, that a Flatlander, seeing a Line, sees something that must be thick to the eye as well as long to the eye (otherwise it would not be visible, if it had not some thickness); and consequently he ought (it is argued) to acknowledge that his countrymen are not only long and broad, but also (though doubtless in a very slight degree) thick or high. This objection is plausible, and, to Space-landers, almost irresistible, so that, I confess, when I first heard it, I knew not what to reply. But my poor old friend's answer appears to me completely to meet it.

"I admit," said he—when I mentioned to him this objection—"I admit the truth of your critic's facts, but I deny his conclusions. It is true that we have really in Flatland a Third unrecognized Dimension called 'height,' just as it is also true that you have really in Spaceland a Fourth unrecognized Dimension, called by no name at present, but which I will call 'extra-height'. But we can no more take cognizance of our 'height' than you can of your 'extra-height'. Even I—who have been in Spaceland, and have had the privilege of understanding for twenty-four hours the meaning of 'height'—even I cannot now compre-hend it, nor realize it by the sense of sight or by any process of reason; I can but apprehend it by faith.

"The reason is obvious. Dimension implies direction, implies measurement, implies the more and the less. Now, all our lines are equally and infinitesimally thick (or high, whichever you like); consequently, there is nothing in them to lead our minds to the conception of that Dimension. No 'delicate micro-meter'—as has been suggested by one too hasty Spaceland critic—would in the least avail us; for we should not know what to measure, nor in what direction. When we see a Line, we see something that is long and bright; brightness, as well as length, is necessary to the existence of a Line; if the brightness vanishes, the Line is extinguished. Hence, all my Flatland friends—when I talk to them about the unrecognized Dimension which is somehow visible in a Line—say, 'Ah, you mean brightness': and when I

reply, 'No, I mean a real Dimension,' they at once retort 'Then measure it, or tell us in what direction it extends'; and this silences me, for I can do neither. Only yesterday, when the Chief Circle (in other words our High Priest) came to inspect the State Prison and paid me his seventh annual visit, and when for the seventh time he put me the question, 'Was I any better?' I tried to prove to him that he was 'high,' as well as long and broad, although he did not know it. But what was his reply? 'You say I am "high"; measure my "high-ness" and I will believe you.' What could I do? How could I meet his challenge? I was crushed; and he left the room triumphant.

"Does this still seem strange to you? Then put yourself in a similar position. Suppose a person of the Fourth Dimension, condescending to visit you, were to say, 'Whenever you open your eyes, you see a Plane (which is of Two Dimensions) and you infer a Solid (which is of Three); but in reality you also see (though you do not recognize) a Fourth Dimension, which is not colour nor brightness nor anything of the kind, but a true Dimension, although I cannot point out to you its direction, nor can you possibly measure it.' What would you say to such a visitor? Would not you have him locked up? Well, that is my fate: and it is as natural for us Flatlanders to lock up a Square for preaching the Third Dimension, as it is for you Spacelanders to lock up a Cube for preaching the Fourth. Alas, how strong a family likeness runs through blind and persecuting humanity in all Dimensions! Points, Lines, Squares, Cubes, Extra-Cubes—we are all liable to the same errors, all alike the Slaves of our respective Dimensional prejudices, as one of your Spaceland poets has said—

'One touch of Nature makes all worlds akin'.*"*[1]

On this point the defence of the Square seems to me to be impregnable. I wish I could say that his answer to the second (or moral) objection was equally clear and cogent. It has been objected that he is a woman-hater; and as this objection has been vehemently urged by those whom Nature's decree has constituted the somewhat larger half of the Spaceland race, I should like to remove it, so far as I can honestly do so. But the Square is so unaccustomed to the use of the moral terminology of Spaceland that I should be doing him an injustice if I were literally to transcribe his defence against this charge. Acting, therefore, as his interpreter and summarizer, I gather that in the course of an imprisonment of seven years he has himself modified his own personal views, both as regards Women and as regards the Isosceles or Lower Classes. Personally, he now inclines to the opinion of the Sphere that the Straight Lines are in many important respects superior to the Circles. But, writing as a Historian, he has identified himself (perhaps too closely) with the views generally adopted by Flatland, and (as he has been informed) even by Spaceland, Historians; in whose pages (until very recent times) the destinies of Women and of the masses of mankind have seldom been deemed worthy of mention and never of careful consideration.

In a still more obscure passage he now desires to disavow the Circular or aristocratic tendencies with which some critics have naturally credited him. While

---

[1] The Author desires me to add, that the misconception of some of his critics on this matter has induced him to insert in his dialogue with the Sphere, certain remarks which have a bearing on the point in question, and which he had previously omitted as being tedious and unnecessary.

doing justice to the intellectual power with which a few Circles have for many generations maintained their supremacy over immense multitudes of their countrymen, he believes that the facts of Flatland, speaking for themselves without comment on his part, declare that Revolutions cannot always be suppressed by slaughter, and that Nature, in sentencing the Circles to infecundity, has condemned them to ultimate failure—"and herein," he says, "I see a fulfilment of the great Law of all worlds, that while the wisdom of Man thinks it is working one thing, the wisdom of Nature constrains it to work another, and quite a different and far better thing." For the rest, he begs his readers not to suppose that every minute detail in the daily life of Flatland must needs correspond to some other detail in Spaceland; and yet he hopes that, taken as a whole, his work may prove suggestive as well as amusing, to those Spacelanders of moderate and modest minds who—speaking of that which is of the highest importance, but lies beyond experience—decline to say on the one hand, "This can never be," and on the other hand, "It must needs be precisely thus, and we know all about it."

CONTENTS

PART I: THIS WORLD

Section

PART II: OTHER WORLDS

PART I
THIS WORLD
"Be patient, for the world is broad and wide."

1.—Of the Nature of Flatland

I call our world Flatland, not because we call it so, but to make its nature clearer to you, my happy readers, who are privileged to live in Space.

Imagine a vast sheet of paper on which straight Lines, Triangles, Squares, Pentagons, Hexagons, and other figures, instead of remaining fixed in their places, move freely about, on or in the surface, but without the power of rising above or sinking below it, very much like shadows—only hard and with luminous edges—and you will then have a pretty correct notion of my country and countrymen. Alas, a few years ago, I should have said "my universe": but now my mind has been opened to higher views of things.

In such a country, you will perceive at once that it is impossible that there should be anything of what you call a "solid" kind; but I dare say you will suppose that we could at least distinguish by sight the Triangles, Squares, and other figures, moving about as I have described them. On the contrary, we could see nothing of the kind, not at least so as to distinguish one figure from another. Nothing was visible, nor could be visible, to us, except Straight Lines; and the necessity of this I will speedily demonstrate.

Place a penny on the middle of one of your tables in Space; and leaning over it, look down upon it. It will appear a circle.

But now, drawing back to the edge of the table, gradually lower your eye (thus bringing yourself more and more into the condition of the inhabitants of Flatland), and you will find the penny becoming more and more oval to your view; and at last when you have placed your eye exactly on the edge of the table (so that you are, as it were, actually a Flatlander) the penny will then have ceased to appear oval at all, and will have become, so far as you can see, a straight line.

The same thing would happen if you were to treat in the same way a Triangle, or Square, or any other figure cut out of pasteboard. As soon as you look at it with your eye on the edge on the table, you will find that it ceases to appear to you a figure, and that it becomes in appearance a straight line. Take for example an equilateral Triangle—who represents with us a Tradesman of the respectable class. Fig. 1 represents the Tradesman as you would see him while you were bending over him from above; figs. 2 and 3 represent the Tradesman, as you would see him if your eye were close to the level, or all but on the level of the table; and if your eye were quite on the level of the table (and that is how we see him in Flatland) you would see nothing but a straight line.

When I was in Spaceland I heard that your sailors have very similar experiences while they traverse your seas and discern some distant island or coast lying on the horizon. The far-off land may have bays, forelands, angles in and out to any number and extent; yet at a distance you see none of these (unless indeed your sun shines bright upon them revealing the pro-

jections and retirements by means of light and shade),
nothing but a grey unbroken line upon the water.

Well, that is just what we see when one of our
triangular or other acquaintances comes toward us in
Flatland. As there is neither sun with us, nor any
light of such a kind as to make shadows, we have
none of the helps to the sight that you have in
Spaceland. If our friend comes closer to us we see
his line becomes larger; if he leaves us it becomes
smaller: but still he looks like a straight line; be he a
Triangle, Square, Pentagon, Hexagon, Circle, what
you will—a straight Line he looks and nothing else.

You may perhaps ask how under these disadvanta-
geous circumstances we are able to distinguish our
friends from one another: but the answer to this very
natural question will be more fitly and easily given
when I come to describe the inhabitants of Flatland.
For the present let me defer this subject, and say a
word or two about the climate and houses in our
country.

2.—Of the Climate and Houses in Flatland

As with you, so also with us, there are four points of the compass North, South, East, and West.

There being no sun nor other heavenly bodies, it is impossible for us to determine the North in the usual way; but we have a method of our own. By a Law of Nature with us, there is a constant attraction to the South; and, although in temperate climates this is very slight—so that even a Woman in reasonable health can journey several furlongs northward without much difficulty—yet the hampering effect of the southward attraction is quite sufficient to serve as a compass in most parts of our earth. Moreover, the rain (which falls at stated intervals) coming always from the North, is an additional assistance; and in the towns we have the guidance of the houses, which of course have their side-walls running for the most part North and South, so that the roofs may keep off the rain from the North. In the country, where there are no houses, the trunks of the trees serve as some sort of guide. Altogether, we have not so much difficulty as might be expected in determining our bearings.

Yet in our more temperate regions, in which the southward attraction is hardly felt, walking sometimes in a perfectly desolate plain where there have been no houses nor trees to guide me, I have been

occasionally compelled to remain stationary for hours
together, waiting till the rain came before continuing
my journey. On the weak and aged, and especially
on delicate Females, the force of attraction tells much
more heavily than on the robust of the Male Sex, so
that it is a point of breeding, if you meet a Lady in
the street, always to give her the North side of the
way—by no means an easy thing to do always at
short notice when you are in rude health and in a
climate where it is difficult to tell your North from
your South.

Windows there are none in our houses: for the
light comes to us alike in our homes and out of them,
by day and by night, equally at all times and in all
places, whence we know not. It was in old days, with
our learned men, an interesting and oft-investigated
question, "What is the origin of light?" and the solution of it has been repeatedly attempted, with no
other result than to crowd our lunatic asylums with
the would-be solvers. Hence, after fruitless attempts
to suppress such investigations indirectly by making
them liable to a heavy tax, the Legislature, in comparatively recent times, absolutely prohibited them.
I—alas, I alone in Flatland—know now only too well
the true solution of this mysterious problem; but my
knowledge cannot be made intelligible to a single
one of my countrymen; and I am mocked at—I, the
sole possessor of the truths of Space and of the
theory of the introduction of Light from the world of
three Dimensions—as if I were the maddest of the
mad! But a truce to these painful digressions: let me
return to our houses.

The most common form for the construction of a
house is five-sided or pentagonal, as in the annexed
figure. The two Northern sides RO, OF, constitute
the roof, and for the most part have no doors; on the

East is a small door for the Women; on the West a much larger one for the Men; the South side or floor is usually doorless.

Square and triangular houses are not allowed, and for this reason. The angles of a Square (and still more those of an equilateral Triangle,) being much more pointed than those of a Pentagon, and the lines of inanimate objects (such as houses) being dimmer than the lines of Men and Women, it follows that there is no little danger lest the points of a square or triangular house residence might do serious injury to an inconsiderate or perhaps absent-minded traveller suddenly therefore, running against them: and as early as the eleventh century of our era, triangular houses were universally forbidden by Law, the only exceptions being fortifications, powder-magazines, barracks, and other state buildings, which it is not desirable that the general public should approach without circumspection.

At this period, square houses were still everywhere permitted, though discouraged by a special tax. But, about three centuries afterwards, the Law decided that in all towns containing a population above ten thousand, the angle of a Pentagon was the smallest house-angle that could be allowed consistently with the public safety. The good sense of the community has seconded the efforts of the Legislature; and now, even in the country, the pentagonal construction has superseded every other. It is only now and then in some very remote and backward agricultural district that an antiquarian may still discover a square house.

3.—Concerning the Inhabitants of Flatland

The greatest length or breadth of a full grown inhabitant of Flatland may be estimated at about eleven of your inches. Twelve inches may be regarded as a maximum.

Our Women are Straight Lines.

Our Soldiers and Lowest Classes of Workmen are Triangles with two equal sides, each about eleven inches long, and a base or third side so short (often not exceeding half an inch) that they form at their vertices a very sharp and formidable angle. Indeed when their bases are of the most degraded type (not more than the eighth part of an inch in size), they can hardly be distinguished from Straight Lines or Women; so extremely pointed are their vertices. With us, as with you, these Triangles are distinguished from others by being called Isosceles; and by this name I shall refer to them in the following pages.

Our Middle Class consists of Equilateral or Equal-Sided Triangles.

Our Professional Men and Gentlemen are Squares (to which class I myself belong) and Five-Sided Figures or Pentagons.

Next above these come the Nobility, of whom there are several degrees, beginning at Six-Sided Figures, or Hexagons, and from thence rising in the number of their sides till they receive the honourable title of Polygonal, or many-sided. Finally when the number of the sides becomes so numerous, and the sides themselves so small, that the figure cannot be distinguished from a circle, he is included in the Circular or Priestly order; and this is the highest class of all.

It is a Law of Nature with us that a male child shall have one more side than his father, so that each generation shall rise (as a rule) one step in the scale of development and nobility. Thus the son of a Square is a Pentagon; the son of a Pentagon, a Hexagon; and so on.

But this rule applies not always to the Tradesmen, and still less often to the Soldiers, and to the Workmen; who indeed can hardly be said to deserve the name of human Figures, since they have not all their sides equal. With them therefore the Law of Nature does not hold; and the son of an Isosceles (*i.e.* a Triangle with two sides equal) remains Isosceles still. Nevertheless, all hope is not shut out, even from the Isosceles, that his posterity may ultimately rise above his degraded condition. For, after a long series of military successes, or diligent and skilful labours, it is generally found that the more intelligent among the Artisan and Soldier classes manifest a slight increase of their third side or base, and a shrinkage of the two other sides. Intermarriages (arranged by the Priests) between the sons and daughters of these more intellectual members of the lower classes generally result in an offspring approximating still more to the type of the Equal-Sided Triangle.

Rarely—in proportion to the vast numbers of Isosceles births—is a genuine and certifiable Equal-Sided

Triangle produced from Isosceles parents.[1] Such a
birth requires, as its antecedents, not only a series of
carefully arranged intermarriages, but also a long,
continued exercise of frugality and self-control on the
part of the would-be ancestors of the coming Equilateral, and a patient, systematic, and continuous
development of the Isosceles intellect through many
generations.

The birth of a True Equilateral Triangle from Isosceles parents is the subject of rejoicing in our country for many furlongs around. After a strict examination
conducted by the Sanitary and Social Board, the
infant, if certified as Regular, is with solemn ceremo-
nial admitted into the class of Equilaterals. He is
then immediately taken from his proud yet sorrow-
ing parents and adopted by some childless Equilateral,
who is bound by oath never to permit the child
henceforth to enter his former home or so much as to
look upon his relations again, for fear lest the freshly
developed organism may, by force of unconscious
imitation, fall back again into his hereditary level.

The occasional emergence of an Equilateral from
the ranks of his serf-born ancestors is welcomed, not
only by the poor serfs themselves, as a gleam of light
and hope shed upon the monotonous squalor of their
existence, but also by the Aristocracy at large; for all
the higher classes are well aware that these rare
phenomena, while they do little or nothing to vulgar-

[1]"What need of a certificate?" a Spaceland critic may ask: "Is not
the procreation of a Square Son a certificate from Nature herself,
proving the Equal-sidedness of the Father?" I reply that no Lady of
any position will marry an uncertified Triangle. Square offspring has
sometimes resulted from a slightly Irregular Triangle; but in almost
every such case the Irregularity of the first generation is visited on
the third; which either fails to attain the Pentagonal rank, or relapses
to the Triangular.

ize their own privileges, serve as a most useful barrier against revolution from below.

Had the acute-angled rabble been all, without
exception, absolutely destitute of hope and of ambition,
they might have found leaders in some of their many
seditious outbreaks, so able as to render their superior numbers and strength too much even for the
wisdom of the Circles. But a wise ordinance of Nature has decreed that, in proportion as the working-
classes increase in intelligence, knowledge, and all
virtue, in that same proportion their acute angle
(which makes them physically terrible) shall increase
also and approximate to the comparatively harmless
angle of the Equilateral Triangle. Thus, in the most
brutal and formidable of the soldier class—creatures
almost on a level with women in their lack of
intelligence—it is found that, as they wax in the
mental ability necessary to employ their tremendous
penetrating power to advantage, so do they wane in
the power of penetration itself.

How admirable is this Law of Compensation! And
how perfect a proof of the natural fitness and, I may
almost say, the divine origin of the aristocratic constitution of the States in Flatland! By a judicious use of
this Law of Nature, the Polygons and Circles are
almost always able to stifle sedition in its very cradle,
taking advantage of the irrepressible and boundless
hopefulness of the human mind. Art also comes to
the aid of Law and Order. It is generally found
possible—by a little artificial compression or expansion on the part of the State physicians—to make
some of the more intelligent leaders of a rebellion
perfectly Regular, and to admit them at once into the
privileged classes; a much larger number, who are
still below the standard, allured by the prospect of
being ultimately ennobled, are induced to enter the

State Hospitals, where they are kept in honourable confinement for life; one or two alone of the more obstinate, foolish, and hopelessly irregular are led to execution.

Then the wretched rabble of the Isosceles, planless and leaderless, are either transfixed without resistance by the small body of their brethren whom the Chief Circle keeps in pay for emergencies of this kind; or else more often, by means of jealousies and suspicions skilfully fomented among them by the Circular party, they are stirred to mutual warfare, and perish by one another's angles. No less than one hundred and twenty rebellions are recorded in our annals, besides minor outbreaks numbered at two hundred and thirty-five; and they have all ended thus.

4.—Concerning the Women.

If our highly pointed Triangles of the Soldier class are formidable, it may be readily inferred that far more formidable are our Women. For if a Soldier is a wedge, a Woman is a needle; being, so to speak, *all* point, at least at the two extremities. Add to this the power of making herself partically invisible at will, and you will perceive that a Female, in Flatland, is a creature by no means to be trifled with.

But here, perhaps, some of my younger Readers may ask *how* a woman in Flatland can make herself invisible. This ought, I think, to be apparent without any explanation. However, a few words will make it clear to the most unreflecting.

Place a needle on a table. Then, with your eye on the level of the table, look at it side-ways, and you see the whole length of it; but look at it end-ways, and you see nothing but a point, it has become practically invisible. Just so is it with one of our Women. When her side is turned towards us, we see her as a straight line; when the end containing her eye or mouth—for with us these two organs are identical—is the part that meets our eye, then we see nothing but a highly lustrous point; but when the back is presented to our view, then—being only sub-lustrous, and, indeed, almost as dim as an inanimate object—her hinder extremity serves her as a kind of Invisible Cap.

The dangers to which we are exposed from our Women must now be manifest to the meanest capacity in Spaceland. If even the angle of a respectable Triangle in the middle class is not without its dangers; if to run against a Working Man involves a gash; if collision with an officer of the military class necessitates a serious wound; if a mere touch from the vertex of a Private Soldier brings with it danger of death;—what can it be to run against a Woman, except absolute and immediate destruction? And when a Woman is invisible, or visible only as a dim sublustrous point, how difficult must it be, even for the most cautious, always to avoid collision!

Many are the enactments made at different times in the different States of Flatland, in order to minimize this peril; and in the Southern and less temperate climates where the force of gravitation is greater, and human beings more liable to casual and involuntary motions, the Laws concerning Women are naturally much more stringent. But a general view of the Code may be obtained from the following summary:—

1. Every house shall have one entrance in the Eastern side, for the use of Females only; by which all females shall enter "in a becoming and respectful manner"[1] and not by the Men's or Western door.

2. No Female shall walk in any public place without continually keeping up her Peace-cry, under penalty of death.

[1]When I was in Spaceland I understood that some of your Priestly circles have in the same way a separate entrance for Villagers, Farmers and Teachers of Board Schools (*Spectator*, Sept. 1884, p. 1255) that they may "approach in a becoming and respectful manner."

3. Any Female, duly certified to be suffering from St. Vitus's Dance, fits, chronic cold accompanied by violent sneezing, or any disease necessitating involuntary motions, shall be instantly destroyed.

In some of the States there is an additional Law forbidding Females, under penalty of death, from walking or standing in any public place without moving their backs constantly from right to left so as to indicate their presence to those behind them; others oblige a Woman, when travelling, to be followed by one of her sons, or servants, or by her husband; others confine Women altogether to their houses except during the religious festivals. But it has been found by the wisest of our Circles or Statesmen that the multiplication of restrictions on Females tends not only to the debilitation and diminution of the race, but also to the increase of domestic murders to such an extent that a State loses more than it gains by a too prohibitive Code.

For whenever the temper of the Women is thus exasperated by confinement at home or hampering regulations abroad, they are apt to vent their spleen upon their husbands and children; and in the less temperate climates the whole male population of a village has been sometimes destroyed in one or two hours of simultaneous female outbreak. Hence the Three Laws, mentioned above, suffice for the better regulated States, and may be accepted as a rough exemplification of our Female Code.

After all, our principal safeguard is found, not in Legislature, but in the interests of the Women themselves. For, although they can inflict instantaneous death by a retrograde movement, yet unless they can at once disengage their stinging extremity from the struggling body of their victim, their own frail bodies are liable to be shattered.

The power of Fashion is also on our side. I pointed out that in some less civilized States no female is suffered to stand in any public place without swaying her back from right to left. This practice has been universal among ladies of any pretensions to breeding in all well-governed States, as far back as the memory of Figures can reach. It is considered a disgrace to any State that legislation should have to enforce what ought to be, and is in every respectable female, a natural instinct. The rhythmical and, if I may so say, well-modulated undulation of the back in our ladies of Circular rank is envied and imitated by the wife of a common Equilateral, who can achieve nothing beyond a mere monotonous swing, like the ticking of a pendulum; and the regular tick of the Equilateral is no less admired and copied by the wife of the progressive and aspiring Isosceles, in the females of whose family no "back-motion" of any kind has become as yet a necessity of life. Hence, in every family of position and consideration, "back motion" is as prevalent as time itself; and the husbands and sons in these households enjoy immunity at least from invisible attacks.

Not that it must be for a moment supposed that our Women are destitute of affection. But unfortunately the passion of the moment predominates, in the Frail Sex, over every other consideration. This is, of course, a necessity arising from their unfortunate conformation. For as they have no pretensions to an angle, being inferior in this respect to the very lowest of the Isosceles, they are consequently wholly devoid of brain-power, and have neither reflection, judgment nor forethought, and hardly any memory. Hence, in their fits of fury, they remember no claims

and recognize no distinctions. I have actually known
a case where a Woman has exterminated her whole
household, and half an hour afterwards, when her
rage was over and the fragments swept away, has
asked what has become of her husband and her
children.

Obviously then a Woman is not to be irritated as
long as she is in a position where she can turn round.
When you have them in their apartments—which
are constructed with a view to denying them that
power—you can say and do what you like; for they
are then wholly impotent for mischief, and will not
remember a few minutes hence the incident for which
they may be at this moment threatening you with
death, nor the promises which you may have found it
necessary to make in order to pacify their fury.

On the whole we get on pretty smoothly in our
domestic relations, except in the lower strata of the
Military Classes. There the want of tact and discretion on the part of the husbands produces at times
indescribable disasters. Relying too much on the of-
fensive weapons of their acute angles instead of the
defensive organs of good sense and seasonable
simulation, these reckless creatures too often neglect
the prescribed construction of the women's apartments, or irritate their wives by ill-advised expressions out of doors, which they refuse immediately to
retract. Moreover a blunt and stolid regard for literal
truth indisposes them to make those lavish promises
by which the more judicious Circle can in a moment
pacify his consort. The result is massacre; not,
however, without its advantages, as it eliminates the
more brutal and troublesome of the Isosceles; and by
many of our Circles the destructiveness of the Thin-
ner Sex is regarded as one among many providential

arrangements for suppressing redundant population, and nipping Revolution in the bud.

Yet even in our best regulated and most approximately Circular families I cannot say that the ideal of family life is so high as with you in Spaceland. There is peace, in so far as the absence of slaughter may be called by that name, but there is necessarily little harmony of tastes or pursuits; and the cautious wisdom of the Circles has ensured safety at the cost of domestic comfort. In every Circular or Polygonal household it has been a habit from time immemorial—and now has become a kind of instinct among the women of our higher classes—that the mothers and daughters should constantly keep their eyes and mouths towards their husband and his male friends; and for a lady in a family of distinction to turn her back upon her husband would be regarded as a kind of portent, involving loss of *status*. But, as I shall soon shew, this custom, though it has the advantage of safety, is not without its disadvantages.

In the house of the Working Man or respectable Tradesman—where the wife is allowed to turn her back upon her husband, while pursuing her household avocations—there are at least intervals of quiet, when the wife is neither seen nor heard, except for the humming sound of the continuous Peace-cry; but in the homes of the upper classes there is too often no peace. There the voluble mouth and bright penetrating eye are ever directed towards the Master of the household; and light itself is not more persistent than the stream of feminine discourse. The tact and skill which suffice to avert a Woman's sting are unequal to the task of stopping a Woman's mouth; and as the wife has absolutely nothing to say, and absolutely no constraint of wit, sense, or conscience to prevent her from saying it, not a few cynics have been found to aver that they prefer the danger of the death-dealing but inaudible sting to the safe sonorousness of a Woman's other end.

To my readers in Spaceland the condition of our Women may seem truly deplorable, and so indeed it is. A Male of the lowest type of the Isosceles may look forward to some improvement of his angle, and to the ultimate elevation of the whole of his degraded caste; but no Woman can entertain such hopes for her sex. "Once a Woman, always a Woman" is a Decree of Nature; and the very Laws of Evolution seem suspended in her disfavour. Yet at least we can admire the wise Prearrangement which has ordained that, as they have no hopes, so they shall have no memory to recall, and no forethought to anticipate, the miseries and humiliations which are at once a necessity of their existence and the basis of the constitution of Flatland.

5.—Of our Methods of Recognizing one another.

You, who are blessed with shade as well as light, you, who are gifted with two eyes, endowed with a knowledge of perspective, and charmed with the enjoyment of various colours, you, who can actually *see* an angle, and contemplate the complete circumference of a circle in the happy region of the Three Dimensions—how shall I make clear to you the extreme difficulty which we in Flatland experience in recognizing one another's configuration?

Recall what I told you above. All beings in Flatland, animate or inanimate, no matter what their form, present *to our view* the same, or nearly the same, appearance, viz. that of a straight Line. How then can one be distinguished from another, where all appear the same?

The answer is threefold. The first means of recognition is the sense of hearing; which with us is far more highly developed than with you, and which enables us not only to distinguish by the voice our personal friends, but even to discriminate between different classes, at least so far as concerns the three lowest orders, the Equilateral, the Square, and the Pentagon —for of the Isosceles I take no account. But as we ascend in the social scale, the process of discriminating and being discriminated by hearing increases in difficulty, partly because voices are assimilated, partly because the faculty of voice-discrimination is a plebeian virtue not much developed among the Aristocracy. And wherever there is any danger of imposture we cannot trust to this method. Amongst our lowest orders, the vocal organs are developed to a degree more than correspondent with those of hearing, so that an Isosceles can easily feign the voice of a Polygon, and, with some training, that of a Circle himself. A second method is therefore more commonly resorted to.

Feeling is, among our Women and lower classes—about our upper classes I shall speak presently—the principal test of recognition, at all events between strangers, and when the question is, not as to the individual, but as to the class. What therefore "introduction" is among the higher classes in Spaceland, that the process of "feeling" is with us. "Permit me to ask you to feel and be felt by my friend Mr. So-and-so"—is still, among the more old-fashioned of our country gentlemen in districts remote from towns, the customary formula for a Flatland introduction. But in the towns, and among men of business, the words "be felt by" are omitted and the sentence is abbreviated to, "Let me ask you to feel Mr. So-and-so"; although it is assumed, of course, that the "feeling" is to be reciprocal. Among our still more modern and dashing young gentlemen—who are extremely averse to superfluous effort and supremely indifferent to the purity of their native language—the formula is still further curtailed by the use of "to feel" in a technical sense, meaning, "to recommend-for-the-purposes-of-feeling-and-being-felt"; and at this moment the "slang" of polite or fast society in the upper classes sanctions such a barbarism as "Mr. Smith, permit me to feel Mr. Jones."

Let not my Reader however suppose that "feeling"

is with us the tedious process that it would be with you, or that we find it necessary to feel right round all the sides of every individual before we determine the class to which he belongs. Long practice and training, begun in the schools and continued in the experience of daily life, enable us to discriminate at once by the sense of touch, between the angles of an equal-sided Triangle, Square, and Pentagon; and I need not say that the brainless vertex of an acute-angled Isosceles is obvious to the dullest touch. It is therefore not necessary, as a rule, to do more than feel a single angle of an individual; and this, once ascertained, tells us the class of the person whom we are addressing, unless indeed he belongs to the higher sections of the nobility. There the difficulty is much greater. Even a Master of Arts in our University of Wentbridge has been known to confuse a ten-sided with a twelve-sided Polygon; and there is hardly a Doctor of Science in or out of that famous University who could pretend to decide promptly and unhesitatingly between a twenty-sided and a twenty-four sided member of the Aristocracy.

Those of my readers who recall the extracts I gave above from the Legislative code concerning Women, will readily perceive that the process of introduction by contact requires some care and discretion. Otherwise the angles might inflict on the unwary Feeler irreparable injury. It is essential for the safety of the Feeler that the Felt should stand perfectly still. A start, a fidgety shifting of the position, yes, even a violent sneeze, has been known before now to prove fatal to the incautious, and to nip in the bud many a promising friendship. Especially is this true among the lower classes of the Triangles. With them, the eye is situated so far from their vertex that they can scarcely take cognizance of what goes on at that

extremity of their frame. They are, moreover, of a
rough coarse nature, not sensitive to the delicate
touch of the highly organized Polygon. What wonder
then if an involuntary toss of the head has ere now
deprived the State of a valuable life!

I have heard that my excellent Grandfather—one
of the least irregular of his unhappy Isosceles class,
who indeed obtained, shortly before his decease,
four out of seven votes from the Sanitary and Social
Board for passing him into the class of the Equal-
sided—often deplored, with a tear in his venerable
eye, a miscarriage of this kind, which had occured to
his great-great-great-Grandfather, a respectable Working Man with an angle or brain of 59°30'. According to
his account, my unfortunate Ancestor, being afflicted
with rheumatism, and in the act of being felt by a
Polygon, by one sudden start accidentally transfixed
the Great Man through the diagonal; and thereby,
partly in consequence of his long imprisonment and
degradation, and partly because of the moral shock
which pervaded the whole of my Ancestor's relations,
threw back our family a degree and a half in their
ascent towards better things. The result was that in
the next generation the family brain was registered
at only 58°, and not till the lapse of five generations
was the lost ground recovered, the full 60° attained,
and the Ascent from the Isosceles finally achieved.
And all this series of calamities from one little accident in the process of Feeling.

At this point I think I hear some of my better
educated readers exclaim, "How could you in Flatland
know anything about angles and degrees, or minutes?
We can *see* an angle, because we, in the region of
Space, can see two straight lines inclined to one
another; but you, who can see nothing but one straight
line at a time, or at all events only a number of bits

of straight lines all in one straight line—how can you ever discern any angle, and much less register angles of different sizes?"

I answer that though we cannot *see* angles, we can *infer* them, and this with great precision. Our sense of touch, stimulated by necessity, and developed by long training, enables us to distinguish angles far more accurately than your sense of sight, when unaided by a rule ōr measure of angles. Nor must I omit to explain that we have great natural helps. It is with us a Law of Nature that the brain of the Isosceles class shall begin at half a degree, or thirty minutes, and shall increase (if it increases at all) by half a degree in every generation; until the goal of 60° is reached, when the condition of serfdom is quitted, and the freeman enters the class of Regulars.

Consequently, Nature herself supplies us with an ascending scale or Alphabet of angles for half a degree up to 60°, Specimens of which are placed in every Elementary School throughout the land. Owing to occasional retrogressions, to still more frequent moral and intellectual stagnation, and to the extraordinary fecundity of the Criminal and Vagabond Classes, there is always a vast superfluity of individuals of the half degree and single degree class, and a fair abundance of Specimens up to 10°. These are absolutely destitute of civic rights; and a great number of them, not having even intelligence enough for the purposes of warfare, are devoted by the States to the service of education. Fettered immovably so as to remove all possibility of danger, they are placed in the class rooms of our Infant Schools, and there they are utilized by the Board of Education for the purpose of imparting to the offspring of the Middle Classes that tact and intelligence of which these wretched creatures themselves are utterly devoid.

In some States the Specimens are occasionally fed
and suffered to exist for several years; but in the
more temperate and better regulated regions, it is
found in the long run more advantageous for the
educational interests of the young, to dispense with
food, and to renew the Specimens every month—
which is about the average duration of the foodless
existence of the Criminal class. In the cheaper schools,
what is gained by the longer existence of the Speci-
men is lost, partly in the expenditure for food, and
partly in the diminished accuracy of the angles, which
are impaired after a few weeks of constant "feeling."
Nor must we forget to add, in enumerating the advantages of the more expensive system, that it tends,
though slightly yet perceptibly, to the diminution of
the redundant Isosceles population—an object which
every statesman in Flatland constantly keeps in view.
On the whole therefore—although I am not ignorant
that, in many popularly elected School Boards, there
is a reaction in favour of "the cheap system" as it is
called—I am myself disposed to think that this is one
of the many cases in which expense is the truest
economy.

But I must not allow questions of School Board
politics to divert me from my subject. Enough has
been said, I trust, to shew that Recognition by Feeling is not so tedious or indecisive a process as might
have been supposed; and it is obviously more trustworthy than Recognition by hearing. Still there
remains, as has been pointed out above, the objection that this method is not without danger. For this
reason many in the Middle and Lower classes, and
all without exception in the Polygonal and Circular
orders, prefer a third method, the description of
which shall be reserved for the next section.

6.—Of Recognition by Sight

I am about to appear very inconsistent. In previous sections I have said that all figures in Flatland present the appearance of a straight line; and it was added or implied, that it is consequently impossible to distinguish by the visual organ between individuals of different classes: yet now I am about to explain to my Spaceland critics how we are able to recognize one another by the sense of sight.

If however the Reader will take the trouble to refer to the passage in which Recognition by Feeling is stated to be universal, he will find this qualification—"among the lower classes." It is only among the higher classes and in our temperate climates that Sight Recognition is practised.

That this power exists in any regions and for any classes is the result of Fog; which prevails during the greater part of the year in all parts save the torrid zones. That which is with you in Spaceland an unmixed evil, blotting out the landscape, depressing the spirits, and enfeebling the health, is by us recognized as a blessing scarcely inferior to air itself, and as the Nurse of arts and Parent of sciences. But let me explain my meaning, without further eulogies on this beneficent Element.

If Fog were non-existent, all lines would appear equally and indistinguishably clear; and this is actually the case in those unhappy countries in which the atmosphere is perfectly dry and transparent. But werever there is a rich supply of Fog objects that are at a distance, say of three feet, are appreciably dimmer than those at a distance of two feet eleven inches; and the result is that by careful and constant experimental observation of comparative dimness and clearness, we are enabled to infer with great exactness the configuration of the object observed.

An instance will do more than a volume of generalities to make my meaning clear.

Suppose I see two individuals approaching whose rank I wish to ascertain. They are, we will suppose, a Merchant and a Physician, or in other words, an Equilateral Triangle and a Pentagon: how am I to distinguish them?

It will be obvious, to every child in Spaceland who has touched the threshold of Geometrical Studies, that, if I can bring my eye so that its glance may bisect an angle (A) of the approaching stranger, my view will lie as it were evenly between his two sides that are next to me (viz. CA and AB), so that I shall contemplate the two impartially, and both will appear of the same size.

Now in the case of (I) the Merchant, what shall I see? I shall see a straight line DAE, in which the middle point (A) will be very bright because it is nearest to me; but on either side the line will shade away *rapidly into dimness*, because the sides AC and AB *recede rapidly into the fog* and what appear to me as the Merchant's extremities, viz. D and E, will be *very dim indeed*.

On the other hand in the case of (2) the Physician, though I shall here also see a line (D′A′E′) with a bright centre (A′), yet it will shade away *less rapidly* into dimness, because the sides (A′C′,A′B′) *recede less rapidly into the fog:* and what appear to me the Physician's extremities, viz. D′ and E′, will not be *not so dim* as the extremities of the Merchant.

The Reader will probably understand from these two instances how—after a very long training supplemented by constant experience—it is possible for the well-educated classes among us to discriminate with fair accuracy between the middle and lowest orders, by the sense of sight. If my Spaceland Patrons have grasped this general conception, so far as to conceive the possibility of it and not to reject my account as altogether incredible—I shall have attained all I can reasonably expect. Were I to attempt further details I should only perplex. Yet for the sake of the young and inexperienced, who may perchance infer—from the two simple instances I have given above, of the manner in which I should recognize my Father and my Sons—that Recognition by sight is an easy affair, it may be needful to point out that in actual life most of the problems of Sight Recognition are far more subtle and complex.

If for example, when my Father, the Triangle,

approaches me, he happens to present his side to me instead of his angle, then, until I have asked him to rotate, or until I have edged my eye round him, I am for the moment doubtful whether he may not be a Straight Line, or, in other words, a Woman. Again, when I am in the company of one of my two hexagonal Grandsons, contemplating one of his sides (AB) full front, it will be evident from the accompanying diagram that I shall see one whole line (AB) in comparative brightness (shading off hardly at all at the ends) and two smaller lines (CA and BD) dim throughout and shading away into greater dimness towards the extremities C and D.

But I must not give way to the temptation of enlarging on these topics. The meanest mathematician in Spaceland will readily believe me when I assert that the problems of life, which present themselves to the well-educated—when they are themselves in motion, rotating, advancing or retreating, and at the same time attempting to discriminate by the sense of sight between a number of Polygons of high rank moving in different directions, as for example in a ball-room or conversazione—must be of a nature to task the angularity of the most intellectual, and amply justify the rich endowments of the Learned Professors of Geometry, both Static and Kinetic, in the illustrious University of Wentbridge, where the

Science and Art of Sight Recognition are regularly taught to large classes of the *élite* of the States.

It is only a few of the scions of our noblest and wealthiest houses, who are able to give the time and money necessary for the thorough prosecution of this noble and valuable Art. Even to me, a Mathematician of no mean standing, and the Grandfather of two most helpful and perfectly regular Hexagons, to find myself in the midst of a crowd of rotating Polygons of the higher classes, is occasionally very perplexing. And of course to a common Tradesman, or Serf, such a sight is almost as unintelligible as it would be to you, my Reader, were you suddenly transported into our country.

In such a crowd you could see on all sides of you nothing but a Line, apparently straight, but of which the parts would vary irregularly and perpetually in brightness or dimness. Even if you had completed your third year in the Pentagonal and Hexagonal classes in the University, and were perfect in the theory of the subject, you would still find that there was need of many years of experience, before you could move in a fashionable crowd without jostling against your betters, whom it is against etiquette to ask to "feel," and who, by their superior culture and breeding, know all about your movements, while you know very little or nothing about theirs. In a word, to comport oneself with perfect propriety in Polygonal society, one ought to be a Polygon oneself. Such at least is the painful teaching of my experience.

It is astonishing how much the Art—or I may almost call it instinct—of Sight Recognition is developed by the habitual practice of it and by the avoidance of the custom of "Feeling." Just as, with you, the deaf and dumb, if once allowed to gesticulate and to use the hand-alphabet, will never acquire the more difficult but far more valuable art of lipspeech and lip-reading, so it is with us as regards "Seeing" and "Feeling." None who in early life resort to "Feeling" will ever learn "Seeing" in perfection.

For this reason, among our Higher Classes, "Feeling" is discouraged or absolutely forbidden. From the cradle their children, instead of going to the Public Elementary schools (where the art of Feeling is taught,) are sent to higher Seminaries of an exclusive character; and at our illustrious University, to "feel" is regarded as a most serious fault, involving Rustication for the first offence, and Expulsion for the second.

But among the lower classes the art of Sight Recognition is regarded as an unattainable luxury. A common Tradesman cannot afford to let his son spend a third of his life in abstract studies. The children of the poor are therefore allowed to "feel" from their earliest years, and they gain thereby a precocity and an early vivacity which contrast at first most favourably with the inert, undeveloped, and listless behaviour of the half-instructed youths of the Polygonal class; but when the latter have at last completed their University course, and are prepared to put their theory into practice, the change that comes over them may almost be described as a new birth, and in every art, science, and social pursuit they rapidly overtake and distance their Triangular competitors.

Only a few of the Polygonal Class fail to pass the Final Test or Leaving Examination at the University. The condition of the unsuccessful minority is truly pitiable. Rejected from the higher class, they are also despised by the lower. They have neither the matured and systematically trained powers of the Polygonal Bachelors and Masters of Arts, nor yet the native precocity and mercurial versatility of the youthful

Tradesman. The professions, the public services, are closed against them; and though in most States they are not actually debarred from marriage, yet they have the greatest difficulty in forming suitable alliances, as experience shews that the offspring of such unfortunate and ill-endowed parents is generally itself unfortunate, if not positively Irregular.

It is from these specimens of the refuse of our Nobility that the great Tumults and Seditions of past ages have generally derived their leaders; and so great is the mischief thence arising that an increasing minority of our more progressive Statesmen are of opinion that true mercy would dictate their entire suppression, by enacting that all who fail to pass the Final Examination of the University should be either imprisoned for life, or extinguished by a painless death.

But I find myself digressing into the subject of Irregularities, a matter of such vital interest that it demands a separate section.

7.—Concerning Irregular Figures

Throughout the previous pages I have been assuming
—what perhaps should have been laid down at the
beginning as a distinct and fundamental proposition—
that every human being in Flatland is a Regular
Figure, that is to say of regular construction. By this
I mean that a Woman must not only be a line, but a
straight line; that an Artisan or Soldier must have
two of his sides equal; that Tradesmen must have
three sides equal; Lawyers (of which class I am a
humble member), four sides equal, and generally,
that in every Polygon, all the sides must be equal.

The size of the sides would of course depend upon
the age of the individual. A Female at birth would be
about an inch long, while a tall adult Woman might
extend to a foot. As to the Males of every class, it
may be roughly said that the length of an adult's
sides, when added together, is two feet or a little
more. But the size of our sides is not under consideration. I am speaking of the *equality* of sides, and
it does not need much reflection to see that the
whole of the social life in Flatland rests upon the
fundamental fact that Nature wills all Figures to have
their sides equal.

If our sides were unequal our angles might be
unequal. Instead of its being sufficient to feel, or
estimate by sight, a single angle in order to deter-

mine the form of an individual, it would be necessary to ascertain each angle by the experiment of Feeling. But life would be too short for such a tedious grouping. The whole science and art of Sight Recognition would at once perish; Feeling, so far as it is an art, would not long survive; intercourse would become perilous or impossible; there would be an end to all confidence, all forethought; no one would be safe in making the most simple social arrangements; in a word, civilization would relapse into barbarism.

Am I going too fast to carry my Readers with me to these obvious conclusions? Surely a moment's reflection, and a single instance from common life, must convince every one that our whole social system is based upon Regularity, or Equality of Angles. You meet, for example, two or three Tradesmen in the street, whom you recognize at once to be Tradesmen by a glance at their angles and rapidly bedimmed sides, and you ask them to step into your house to lunch. This you do at present with perfect confidence, because everyone knows to an inch or two the area occupied by an adult Triangle: but imagine that your Tradesman drags behind his regular and respectable vertex, a parallelogram of twelve or thirteen inches in diagonal:—what are you to do with such a monster sticking fast in your house door?

But I am insulting the intelligence of my Readers by accumulating details which must be patent to everyone who enjoys the advantages of a Residence in Spaceland. Obviously the measurements of a single angle would no longer be sufficient under such portentious circumstances; one's whole life would be taken up in feeling or surveying the perimeter of one's acquaintances. Already the difficulties of avoiding a collision in a crowd are enough to tax the sagacity of even a well-educated Square; but if no one could calculate the Regularity of a single figure in the company, all would be chaos and confusion, and the slightest panic would cause serious injuries, or—if there happened to be any Women or Soldiers present—perhaps considerable loss of life.

Expediency therefore concurs with Nature in stamping the seal of its approval upon Regularity of conformation: nor has the Law been backward in seconding their efforts. "Irregularity of Figure" means with us the same as, or more than, a combination of moral obliquity and criminality with you, and is treated accordingly. There are not wanting, it is true, some promulgators of paradoxes who maintain that there is no necessary connection between geometrical and moral Irregularity. "The Irregular," they say, "is from his birth scouted by his own parents, derided by his brothers and sisters, neglected by the domestics, scorned and suspected by society, and excluded from all posts of responsibility, trust, and useful activity. His every movement is jealously watched by the police till he comes of age and presents himself for inspection; then he is either destroyed, if he is found to exceed the fixed margin of deviation, or else immured in a Government Office as a clerk of the seventh class; prevented from marriage; forced to drudge at an uninteresting occupation for a miserable stipend; obliged to live and board at the office, and to take even his vacation under close supervision; what wonder that human nature, even in the best and purest, is embittered and perverted by such surroundings!"

All this very plausible reasoning does not convince me, as it has not convinced the wisest of our Statesmen, that our ancestors erred in laying it down as an axiom of policy that the toleration of Irregularity is incompatible with the safety of the State.

Doubtless, the life of an Irregular is hard; but the interests of the Greater Number require that it shall be hard. If a man with a triangular front and a polygonal back were allowed to exist and to propagate a still more Irregular posterity, what would become of the arts of life? Are the houses and doors and churches in Flatland to be altered in order to accommodate such monsters? Are our ticket-collectors to be required to measure every man's perimeter before they allow him to enter a theatre or to take his place in a lecture room? Is an Irregular to be exempted from the militia? And if not, how is he to be prevented from carrying desolation into the ranks of his comrades? Again, what irresistible temptations to fraudulent impostures must needs beset such a creature! How easy for him to enter a shop with his polygonal front foremost, and to order goods to any extent from a confiding tradesman! Let the advocates of a falsely called Philanthropy plead as they may for the abrogation of the Irregular Penal Laws, I for my part have never known an Irregular who was not also what Nature evidently intended him to be—a hypocrite, a misanthropist, and, up to the limits of his power, a perpetrator of all manner of mischief.

Not that I should be disposed to recommend (at present) the extreme measures adopted in some States, where an infant whose angle deviates by half a degree from the correct angularity is summarily destroyed at birth. Some of our highest and ablest men, men of real genius, have during their earliest days laboured under deviations as great as, or even greater than, forty-five minutes: and the loss of their precious lives would have been an irreparable injury to the State. The art of healing also has achieved some of its most glorious triumphs in the compressions, extensions, trepannings, colligations, and other surgi-

cal or diaetetic operations by which Irregularity has
been partly or wholly cured. Advocating therefore a
Via Media, I would lay down no fixed or absolute
line of demarcation; but at the period when the
frame is just beginning to set, and when the Medical
Board has reported that recovery is improbable, I
would suggest that the Irregular offspring be pain-
lessly and mercifully consumed.

8.—Of the Ancient Practice of Painting

If my Readers have followed me with any attention up to this point, they will not be surprised to hear that life is somewhat dull in Flatland. I do not, of course, mean that there are not battles, conspiracies, tumults, factions, and all those other phenomena which are supposed to make History interesting; nor would I deny that the strange mixture of the problems of life and the problems of Mathematics, continually inducing conjecture and giving the opportunity of immediate verification, imparts to our existence a zest which you in Spaceland can hardly comprehend. I speak now from the aesthetic and artistic point of view when I say that life with us is dull; aesthetically and artistically, very dull indeed.

How can it be otherwise, when all one's prospect, all one's landscapes, historical pieces, portraits, flowers, still life, are nothing but a single line, with no varieties except degrees of brightness and obscurity?

It was not always thus. Colour, if Tradition speaks the truth, once for the space of half a dozen centuries or more, threw a transient splendour over the lives of our ancestors in the remotest ages. Some private individual—a Pentagon whose name is variously reported—having casually discovered the constituents of the simpler colours and a rudimentary method of painting, is said to have begun decorating first his house, then his slaves, then his Father, his Sons, and Grandsons, lastly himself. The convenience as well as the beauty of the results commended themselves to all. Wherever Chromatistes,—for by that name the most trustworthy authorities concur in calling him,—turned his variegated frame, there he at once excited attention, and attracted respect. No one now needed to "feel" him; no one mistook his front for his back; all his movements were readily ascertained by his neighbours without the slightest strain on their powers of calculation; no one jostled him, or failed to make way for him; his voice was saved the labour of that exhausting utterance by which we colourless Squares and Pentagons are often forced to proclaim our individuality when we move amid a crowd of ignorant Isosceles.

The fashion spread like wildfire. Before a week was over, every Square and Triangle in the district had copied the example of Chromatistes, and only a few of the more conservative Pentagons still held out. A month or two found even the Dodecagons infected with the innovation. A year had not elapsed before the habit had spread to all but the very highest of the Nobility. Needless to say, the custom soon made its way from the district of Chromatistes to surrounding regions; and within two generations no one in all Flatland was colourless except the Women and the Priests.

Here Nature herself appeared to erect a barrier, and to plead against extending the innovation to these two classes. Many-sidedness was almost essential as a pretext for the Innovators. "Distinction of sides is intended by Nature to imply distinction of colours"—such was the sophism which in those days flew from mouth to mouth, converting whole towns at a time to the new culture. But manifestly to our

Priests and Women this adage did not apply. The latter had only one side, and therefore—plurally and pedantically speaking—*no sides*. The former—if at least they would assert their claim to be really and truly Circles, and not mere high-class Polygons with an infinitely large number of infinitesimally small sides—were in the habit of boasting (what Women confessed and deplored) that they also had no sides, being blessed with a perimeter of one line, or, in other words, a Circumference. Hence it came to pass that these two Classes could see no force in the so-called axiom about "Distinction of Sides implying Distinction of Colour;" and when all others had succumbed to the fascinations of corporal decoration, the Priests and the Women alone still remained pure from the pollution of paint.

Immoral, licentious, anarchical, unscientific—call them by what names you will—yet, from an aesthetic point of view, those ancient days of the Colour Revolt were the glorious childhood of Art in Flatland—a childhood, alas, that never ripened into manhood, nor even reached the blossom of youth. To live was then in itself a delight, because living implied seeing. Even at a small party, the company was a pleasure to behold; the richly varied hues of the assembly in a church or theatre are said to have more than once proved too distracting for our greatest teachers and actors; but most ravishing of all is said to have been the unspeakable magnificence of a military review.

The sight of a line of battle of twenty thousand Isosceles suddenly facing about, and exchanging the sombre black of their bases for the orange and purple of the two sides including their acute angle; the militia of the Equilateral Triangles tricoloured in red, white, and blue; the mauve, ultra-marine, gamboge, and burnt umber of the Square artillerymen rapidly rotating near their vermilion guns; the dashing and flashing of the five-coloured and six-coloured Pentagons and Hexagons careering across the field in their offices of surgeons, geometricians and aides-de-camp— all these may well have been sufficient to render credible the famous story how an illustrious Circle, overcome by the artistic beauty of the forces under his command, threw aside his marshal's bâton and his royal crown, exclaiming that he henceforth exchanged them for the artist's pencil. How great and glorious the sensuous development of these days must have been is in part indicated by the very language and vocabulary of the period. The commonest utterances of the commonest citizens in the time of the Colour Revolt seem to have been suffused with a richer tinge of word or thought; and to that era we are even now indebted for our finest poetry and for whatever rhythm still remains in the more scientific utterance of these modern days.

9.—Of the Universal Colour Bill

But meanwhile the intellectual Arts were fast decaying.

The Art of Sight Recognition, being no longer needed, was no longer practised; and the studies of Geometry, Statics, Kinetics, and other kindred subjects, came soon to be considered superfluous, and fell into disrespect and neglect even at our University. The inferior Art of Feeling speedily experienced the same fate at our Elementary Schools. Then the Isosceles classes, asserting that the Specimens were no longer used nor needed, and refusing to pay the customary tribute from the Criminal classes to the service of Education, waxed daily more numerous and more insolent on the strength of their immunity from the old burden which had formerly exercised the twofold wholesome effect of at once taming their brutal nature and thinning their excessive numbers.

Year by year the Soldiers and Artisans began more vehemently to assert—and with increasing truth—that there was no great difference between them and the very highest class of Polygons, now that they were raised to an equality with the latter, and enabled to grapple with all the difficulties and solve all the problems of life, whether Statical or Kinetical, by the simple process of Colour Recognition. Not content with the natural neglect into which Sight Recognition was falling, they began boldly to demand the legal prohibition of all "monopolizing and aristocratic Arts" and the consequent abolition of all endowments for the studies of Sight Recognition, Mathematics, and Feeling. Soon, they began to insist that inasmuch as Colour, which was a second Nature, had destroyed the need of aristocratic distinctions, the Law should follow in the same path, and that henceforth all individuals and all classes should be recognized as absolutely equal and entitled to equal rights.

Finding the higher Orders wavering and undecided, the leaders of the Revolution advanced still further in their requirements, and at last demanded that all classes alike, the Priests and the Women not excepted, should do homage to Colour by submitting to be painted. When it was objected that Priests and Women had no sides, they retorted that Nature and Expediency concurred in dictating that the front half of every human being (that is to say, the half containing his eye and mouth) should be distinguishable from his hinder half. They therefore brought before a general and extraordinary Assembly of all the States of Flatland a Bill proposing that in every Woman the half containing the eye and mouth should be coloured red, and the other half green. The Priests were to be painted in the same way, red being applied to that semicircle in which the eye and mouth formed the middle point; while the other or hinder semicircle was to be coloured green.

There was no little cunning in this proposal, which indeed emanated not from any Isosceles—for no being so degraded would have had angularity enough to appreciate, must less to devise, such a model of state-craft—but from an Irregular Circle who, instead of being destroyed in his childhood, was reserved by a foolish indulgence to bring desolation on his country and destruction on myriads of his followers.

On the one hand the proposition was calculated to bring the Women in all classes over to the side of the Chromatic Innovation. For by assigning to the Women the same two colours as were assigned to the Priests, the Revolutionists thereby ensured that, in certain positions, every Woman would appear like a Priest, and be treated with corresponding respect and deference—a prospect that could not fail to attract the Female Sex in a mass.

But by some of my Readers the possibility of the identical appearance of Priests and Women, under the new Legislation, may not be recognized; if so, a word or two will make it obvious.

Imagine a woman duly decorated, according to the new Code; with the front half (*i.e.* the half containing eye and mouth) red, and with the hinder half green. Look at her from one side. Obviously you will see a straight line, *half red, half green*.

Now imagine a Priest, whose mouth is at M, and whose front semicircle (AMB) is consequently coloured red, while his hinder semicircle is green; so that the diameter AB divides the green from the red. If you contemplate the Great Man so as to have your eye in the same straight line as his dividing diameter (AB), what you will see will be a straight line (CBD), of

which *one half* (CB) *will be red, and the other* (BD)
green. The whole line (CD) will be rather shorter
perhaps than that of a full-sized Woman, and will
shade off more rapidly towards its extremities; but
the identity of the colours would give you an immediate impression of identity of Class, making you ne-
glectful of other details. Bear in mind the decay of
Sight Recognition which threatened society at the
time of the Colour Revolt; add too the certainty that
Women would speedily learn to shade off their extremities so as to imitate the Circles; it must then be
surely obvious to you, my dear Reader, that the
Colour Bill placed us under a great danger of con-
founding a Priest with a young Woman.

How attractive this prospect must have been to
the Frail Sex may readily be imagined. They anticipated with delight the confusion that would ensue.
At home they might hear political and ecclesiastical
secrets intended not for them but for their husbands
and brothers, and might even issue commands in the
name of a priestly Circle; out of doors the striking
combination of red and green, without addition of
any other colours, would be sure to lead the common
people into endless mistakes, and the Women would
gain whatever the Circles lost, in the deference of
the passers by. As for the scandal that would befall
the Circular Class if the frivolous and unseemly conduct of the Women were imputed to them, and as to
the consequent subversion of the Constitution, the
Female Sex could not be expected to give a thought
to these considerations. Even in the households of
the Circles, the Women were all in favour of the
Universal Colour Bill.

The second object aimed at by the Bill was the
gradual demoralization of the Circles themselves. In
the general intellectual decay they still preserved

their pristine clearness and strength of understanding. From their earliest childhood, familiarized in their Circular households with the total absence of Colour, the Nobles alone preserved the Sacred Art of Sight Recognition, with all the advantages that result from that admirable training of the intellect. Hence, up to the date of the introduction of the Universal Colour Bill, the Circles had not only held their own, but even increased their lead of the other classes by abstinence from the popular fashion.

Now therefore the artful Irregular whom I described above as the real author of this diabolical Bill, determined at one blow to lower the status of the Hierarchy by forcing them to submit to the pollution of Colour, and at the same time to destroy their domestic opportunities of training in the Art of Sight Recognition, so as to enfeeble their intellects by depriving them of their pure and colourless homes. Once subjected to the chromatic taint, every parental and every childish Circle would demoralize each other. Only in discerning between the Father and the Mother would the Circular infant find problems for the exercise of its understanding—problems too often likely to be corrupted by maternal impostures with the result of shaking the child's faith in all logical conclusions. Thus by degrees the intellectual lustre of the Priestly Order would wane, and the road would then lie open for a total destruction of all Aristocratic Legislature and for the subversion of our Privileged Classes.

10.—Of the Suppression of Chromatic Sedition

The agitation for the Universal Colour Bill continued for three years; and up to the last moment of that period it seemed as though Anarchy were destined to triumph.

A whole army of Polygons, who turned out to fight as private soldiers, was utterly annihilated by a superior force of Isosceles Triangles— the Squares and Pentagons meanwhile remaining neutral. Worse than all, some of the ablest Circles fell a prey to conjugal fury. Infuriated by political animosity, the wives in many a noble household wearied their lords with prayers to give up their opposition to the Colour Bill; and some, finding their entreaties fruitless, fell on and slaughtered their innocent children and husband, perishing themselves in the act of carnage. It is recorded that during that triennial agitation no less than twenty-three Circles perished in domestic discord.

Great indeed was the peril. It seemed as though the Priests had no choice between submission and extermination; when suddenly the course of events was completely changed by one of those picturesque incidents which Statesmen ought never to neglect, often to anticipate, and sometimes perhaps to originate, because of the absurdly disproportionate power with which they appeal to the sympathies of the populace.

It happened that an Isosceles of a low type, with a brain little if at all above four degrees—accidentally dabbling in the colours of some Tradesman whose shop he had plundered—painted himself, or caused himself to be painted (for the story varies) with the twelve colours of a Dodecagon. Going into the Market Place he accosted in a feigned voice a maiden, the orphan daughter of a noble Polygon, whose affection in former days he had sought in vain; and by a series of deceptions—aided, on the one side, by a string of lucky accidents too long to relate, and on the other, by an almost inconceivable fatuity and neglect of ordinary precautions on the part of the relations of the bride—he succeeded in consummating the marriage. The unhappy girl committed suicide on discovering the fraud to which she had been subjected.

When the news of this catastrophe spread from State to State the minds of the Women were violently agitated. Sympathy with the miserable victim and anticipations of similar deceptions for themselves, their sisters, and their daughters, made them now regard the Colour Bill in an entirely new aspect. Not a few openly avowed themselves converted to antagonism; the rest needed only a slight stimulus to make a similar avowal. Seizing this favourable opportunity, the Circles hastily convened an extraordinary Assembly of the States; and besides the usual guard of Convicts, they secured the attendance of a large number of reactionary Women.

Amidst an unprecedented concourse, the Chief Circle of those days—by name Pantocyclus—arose to find himself hissed and hooted by a hundred and twenty thousand Isosceles. But he secured silence by

declaring that henceforth the Circles would enter on
a policy of Concession; yielding to the wishes of the
majority, they would accept the Colour Bill. The
uproar being at once converted to applause, he in-
vited Chromatistes, the leader of the Sedition, into
the centre of the hall, to receive in the name of his
followers the submission of the Hierarchy. Then followed a speech, a masterpiece of rhetoric, which
occupied nearly a day in the delivery, and to which
no summary can do justice.

With a grave appearance of impartiality he declared that as they were now finally committing themselves to Reform or Innovation, it was desirable that
they should take one last view of the perimeter of
the whole subject, its defects as well as its advantages.
Gradually introducing the mention of the dangers to
the Tradesmen, the Professional Classes and the
Gentlemen, he silenced the rising murmurs of the
Isosceles by reminding them that, in spite of all
these defects, he was willing to accept the Bill if it
was approved by the majority. But it was manifest
that all, except the Isosceles, were moved by his
words and were either neutral or averse to the Bill.

Turning now to the Workmen he asserted that
their interests must not be neglected, and that, if
they intended to accept the Colour Bill, they ought
at least to do so with full view of the consequences.
Many of them, he said, were on the point of being
admitted to the class of the Regular Triangles; others
anticipated for their children a distinction they could
not hope for themselves. That honourable ambition
would now have to be sacrificed. With the universal
adoption of Colour, all distinctions would cease; Regularity would be confused with Irregularity; development would give place to retrogression; the Workman
would in a few generations be degraded to the level

of the Military, or even the Convict Class; political power would be in the hands of the greatest number, that is to say the Criminal Classes, who were already more numerous than the Workmen, and would soon out-number all the other Classes put together when the usual Compensative Laws of Nature were violated.

A subdued murmur of assent ran through the ranks of the Artisans, and Chromatistes, in alarm, attempted to step forward and address them. But he found himself encompassed with guards and forced to remain silent while the Chief Circle in a few impassioned words made a final appeal to the Women, exclaiming that, if the Colour Bill passed, no marriage would henceforth be safe, no woman's honour secure; fraud, deception, hypocrisy would pervade every household; domestic bliss would share the fate of the Constitution and pass to speedy perdition. "Sooner than this," he cried, "Come death."

At these words, which were the preconcerted signal for action, the Isosceles Convicts fell on and transfixed the wretched Chromatistes; the Regular Classes, opening their ranks, made way for a band of Women who, under direction of the Circles, moved, back foremost, invisibly and unerringly upon the unconscious soldiers; the Artisans, imitating the example of their betters, also opened their ranks. Meantime bands of Convicts occupied every entrance with an impenetrable phalanx.

The battle, or rather carnage, was of short duration. Under the skillful generalship of the Circles almost every Woman's charge was fatal and very many extracted their sting uninjured, ready for a second slaughter. But no second blow was needed; the rabble of the Isosceles did the rest of the business for themselves. Surprised, leader-less, attacked in front by invisible foes, and finding egress cut off by the

Convicts behind them, they at once—after their manner—lost all presence of mind, and raised the cry of "treachery." This sealed their fate. Every Isosceles now saw and felt a foe in every other. In half an hour not one of that vast multitude was living; and the fragments of seven score thousand of the Criminal Class slain by one another's angles attested the triumph of Order.

The Circles delayed not to push their victory to the uttermost. The Working Men they spared but decimated. The Militia of the Equilaterals was at once called out; and every Triangle suspected of Irregularity on reasonable grounds, was destroyed by Court Martial, without the formality of exact measurement by the Social Board. The homes of the Military and Artisan classes were inspected in a course of visitations extending through upwards of a year; and during that period every town, village, and hamlet was systematically purged of that excess of the lower orders which had been brought about by the neglect to pay the tribute of Criminals to the Schools and University, and by the violation of the other natural Laws of the Constitution of Flatland. Thus the balance of classes was again restored.

Needless to say that henceforth the use of Colour was abolished, and its possession prohibited. Even the utterance of any word denoting Colour, except by the Circles or by qualified scientific teachers, was punished by a severe penalty. Only at our University in some of the very highest and most esoteric classes—which I myself have never been privileged to attend—it is understood that the sparing use of Colour is still sanctioned for the purpose of illustrating some of the deeper problems of mathematics. But of this I can only speak from hearsay.

Elsewhere in Flatland, Colour is now non-existent.

The art of making it is known to only one living
person, the Chief Circle for the time being; and by
him it is handed down on his death-bed to none but
his Successor. One manufactory alone produces it;
and, lest the secret should be betrayed, the Workmen are annually consumed, and fresh ones introduced. So great is the terror with which even now
our Aristocracy looks back to the far-distant days of
the agitation for the Universal Colour Bill.

11.—Concerning our Priests

It is high time that I should pass from these brief and discursive notes about things in Flatland to the central event of this book, my initiation into the mysteries of Space. *That* is my subject; all that has gone before is merely preface.

For this reason I must omit many matters of which the explanation would not, I flatter myself, be without interest for my Readers: as for example, our method of propelling and stopping ourselves, although destitute of feet; the means by which we give fixity to structures of wood, stone, or brick, although of course we have no hands, nor can we lay foundations as you can, nor avail ourselves of the lateral pressure of the earth; the manner in which the rain originates in the intervals between our various zones, so that the northern regions do not intercept the moisture from falling on the southern; the nature of our hills and mines, our trees and vegetables, our seasons and harvests; our Alphabet and method of writing, adapted to our linear tablets; these and a hundred other details of our physical existence I must pass over, nor do I mention them now except to indicate to my readers that their omission proceeds not from forgetfulness on the part of the author, but from his regard for the time of the Reader.

Yet before I proceed to my legitimate subject some

few final remarks will no doubt be expected by my
Readers upon those pillars and mainstays of the Constitution of Flatland, the controllers of our conduct
and shapers of our destiny, the objects of universal
homage and almost of adoration: need I say that I
mean our Circles or Priests?

When I call them Priests, let me not be understood as meaning no more than the term denotes
with you. With us, our Priests are Administrators of
all Business, Art, and Science; Directors of Trade,
Commerce, Generalship, Architecture, Engineering,
Education, Statesmanship, Legislature, Morality,
Theology; doing nothing themselves, they are the
Causes of everything worth doing, that is done by
others.

Although popularly everyone called a Circle is
deemed a Circle, yet among the better educated
Classes it is known that no Circle is really a Circle,
but only a Polygon with a very large number of very
small sides. As the number of the sides increases, a
Polygon approximates to a Circle; and, when the
number is very great indeed, say for example three
or four hundred, it is extremely difficult for the most
delicate touch to feel any polygonal angles. Let me
say rather, it *would* be difficult: for, as I have shown
above, Recognition by Feeling is unknown among
the highest society, and to *feel* a Circle would be
considered a most audacious insult. This habit of
abstention from Feeling in the best society enables a
Circle the more easily to sustain the veil of mystery
in which, from his earliest years, he is wont to en-
wrap the exact nature of his Perimeter or Circumference. Three feet being the average Perimeter it
follows that, in a Polygon of three hundred sides
each side will be no more than the hundredth part of
a foot in length, or little more than the tenth part of

an inch; and in a Polygon of six or seven hundred
sides the sides are little larger than the diameter of a
Spaceland pin-head. It is always assumed, by courtesy,
that the Chief Circle for the time being has ten
thousand sides.

The ascent of the posterity of the Circles in the
social scale is not restricted, as it is among the lower
Regular classes, by the Law of Nature which limits
the increase of sides to one in each generation. If it
were so, the number of sides in a Circle would be a
mere question of pedigree and arithmetic, and the
four hundred and ninety-seventh descendant of an
Equilateral Triangle would necessarily be a Polygon
with five hundred sides. But this is not the case.
Nature's Law prescribes two antagonistic decrees af-
fecting Circular propagation; first, that as the race
climbs higher in the scale of development, so development shall proceed at an accelerated pace; second,
that in the same proportion, the race shall become
less fertile. Consequently in the home of a Polygon
of four or five hundred sides it is rare to find a son;
more than one is never seen. On the other hand the
son of a five-hundred-sided Polygon has been known
to possess five hundred and fifty, or even six hundred sides.

Art also steps in to help the process of the higher
Evolution. Our physicians have discovered that the
small and tender sides of an infant Polygon of the
higher class can be fractured, and his whole frame
re-set, with such exactness that a Polygon of two or
three hundred sides sometimes—by no means always,
for the process is attended with serious risk—but
sometimes overleaps two or three hundred generations, and as it were doubles at a stroke, the number of his progenitors and the nobility of his descent.
Many a promising child is sacrificed in this way.

Scarcely one out of ten survives. Yet so strong is the parental ambition among those Polygons who are, as it were, on the fringe of the Circular class, that it is very rare to find a Nobleman of that position in society, who has neglected to place his first-born in the Circular Neo-Therapeutic Gymnasium before he has attained the age of a month.

One year determines success or failure. At the end of that time the child has, in all probability, added one more to the tombstones that crowd the Neo-Therapeutic Cemetery; but on rare occasions a glad procession bears back the little one to his exultant parents, no longer a Polygon, but a Circle, at least by courtesy: and a single instance of so blessed a result induces multitudes of Polygonal parents to submit to similar domestic sacrifices, which have a dissimilar issue.

12.—Of the Doctrine of our Priests

As to the doctrine of the Circles it may briefly be summed up in a single maxim, "Attend to your Configuration." Whether political, ecclesiastical, or moral, all their teaching has for its object the improvement of individual and collective Configuration—with special reference of course to the Configuration of the Circles, to which all other objects are subordinated.

It is the merit of the Circles that they have effectually suppressed those ancient heresies which led men to waste energy and sympathy in the vain belief that conduct depends upon will, effort, training, encouragement, praise, or anything else but Configuration. It was Pantocyclus—the illustrious Circle mentioned above, as the queller of the Colour Revolt—who first convinced mankind that Configuration makes the man; that if, for example, you are born an Isosceles with two uneven sides, you will assuredly go wrong unless you have them made even—for which purpose you must go to the Isosceles Hospital; similarly, if you are a Triangle, or Square, or even a Polygon, born with any Irregularity, you must be taken to one of the Regular Hospitals to have your disease cured; otherwise you will end your days in the State Prison or by the angle of the State Executioner.

All faults or defects, from the slightest misconduct

to the most flagitious crime, Pantocyclus attributed
to some deviation from perfect Regularity in thè
bodily figure, caused perhaps (if not congenital) by
some collision in a crowd; by neglect to take exercise,
or by taking too much of it; or even by a sudden
change of temperature, resulting in a shrinkage or
expansion in some too susceptible part of the frame.
Therefore, concluded that illustrious Philosopher, neither good conduct nor bad conduct is a fit subject, in
any sober estimation, for either praise or blame. For
why should you praise, for example, the integrity of
a Square who faithfully defends the interests of his
client, when you ought in reality rather to admire
the exact precision of his right angles? Or again, why
blame a lying, thievish Isosceles when you ought
rather to deplore the incurable inequality of his sides?

Theoretically, this doctrine is unquestionable; but
it has practical drawbacks. In dealing with an Isosceles,
if a rascal pleads that he cannot help stealing because
of his unevenness, you reply that for that very reason,
because he cannot help being a nuisance to his
neighbours, you, the Magistrate, cannot help sentencing him to be consumed—and there's an end of
the matter. But in little domestic difficulties, where
the penalty of consumption, or death, is out of the
question, this theory of Configuration sometimes
comes in awkwardly; and I must confess that occasionally when one of my own Hexagonal Grandsons
pleads as an excuse for his disobedience that a sudden change of the temperature has been too much
for his Perimeter, and that I ought to lay the blame
not on him but on his Configuration, which can only
be strengthened by abundance of the choicest sweet-
meats, I neither see my way logically to reject, nor
practically to accept, his conclusions.

For my own part, I find it best to assume that a

good sound scolding or castigation has some latent and strengthening influence on my Grandson's Configuration; though I own that I have no grounds for thinking so. At all events I am not alone in my way of extricating myself from this dilemma; for I find that many of the highest Circles, sitting as Judges in law courts, use praise and blame towards Regular and Irregular Figures; and in their homes I know by experience that, when scolding their children, they speak about "right" or "wrong" as vehemently and passionately as if they believed that these names represented real existences, and that a human Figure is really capable of choosing between them.

Constantly carrying out their policy of making Configuration the leading idea in every mind, the Circles reverse the nature of that Commandment which in Spaceland regulates the relations between parents and children. With you, children are taught to honour their parents; with us—next to the Circles, who are the chief object of universal homage—a man is taught to honour his Grandson, if he has one; or, if not, his Son. By "honour," however, is by no means meant "indulgence," but a reverent regard for their highest interests: and the Circles teach that the duty of fathers is to subordinate their own interests to those of posterity, thereby advancing the welfare of the whole State as well as that of their own immediate descendants.

The weak point in the system of the Circles—if a humble Square may venture to speak of anything Circular as containing any element of weakness— appears to me to be found in their relations with Women.

As it is of the utmost importance for Society that Irregular births should be discouraged, it follows that no Woman who has any Irregularities in her ancestry is a fit partner for one who desires that his posterity should rise by regular degrees in the social scale.

Now the Irregularity of a Male is a matter of measurement; but as all Women are straight, and therefore visibly Regular so to speak, one has to devise some other means of ascertaining what I may call their invisible Irregularity, that is to say their potential Irregularities as regards possible offspring. This is affected by carefully-kept pedigrees, which are preserved and supervised by the State; and without a certified pedigree no Woman is allowed to marry.

Now it might have been supposed that a Circle— proud of his ancestry and regardful for a posterity which might possibly issue hereafter in a Chief Circle—would be more careful than any other to choose a wife who had no blot on her escutcheon. But it is not so. The care in choosing a Regular wife appears to diminish as one rises in the social scale. Nothing would induce an aspiring Isosceles, who had hopes of generating an Equilateral Son, to take a wife who reckoned a single Irregularity among her Ancestors; a Square or Pentagon, who is confident that his family is steadily on the rise, does not inquire above the five-hundredth generation; a Hexagon or Dodecagon is even more careless of the wife's pedigree; but a Circle has been known deliberately to take a wife who has had an Irregular Great-Grandfather, and all because of some slight superiority of lustre, or because of the charms of a low voice—which, with us, even more than you, is thought "an excellent thing in Woman."

Such ill-judged marriages are, as might be expected, barren, if they do not result in positive Irregularity or in diminution of sides; but none of these evils have hitherto proved sufficiently deterrent. The loss of a few sides in a highly-developed Polygon is not easily noticed, and is sometimes compensated by a successful operation in the Neo-Therapeutic Gymnasium, as I have described above; and the Circles are too much disposed to acquiesce in infecundity as a Law of the superior development. Yet, if this evil be not arrested, the gradual diminution of the Circular class may soon become more rapid, and the time may be not far distant when, the race being no longer able to produce a Chief Circle, the Constitution of Flatland must fall.

One other word of warning suggests itself to me, though I cannot so easily mention a remedy; and this also refers to our relations with Women. About three hundred years ago, it was decreed by the Chief Circle that, since women are deficient in Reason but abundant in Emotion, they ought no longer to be treated as rational, nor receive any mental education. The consequence was that they were no longer taught to read, nor even to master Arithmetic enough to enable them to count the angles of their husband or children; and hence they sensibly declined during each generation in intellectual power. And this system of female non-education or quietism still prevails.

My fear is that, with the best intentions, this policy has been carried so far as to react injuriously on the Male Sex.

For the consequence is that, as things now are, we Males have to lead a kind of bi-lingual, and I may almost say bi-mental, existence. With Women, we speak of "love," "duty," "right," "wrong," "pity," "hope," and other irrational and emotional conceptions, which have no existence, and the fiction of which has no object except to control feminine exuberances; but among ourselves, and in our books, we have an entirely different vocabulary and I may almost say, idiom: "Love" then becomes "the anticipation of benefits"; "duty" becomes "necessity", or "fitness"; and other words are correspondingly transmuted. Moreover, among Women, we use language implying the utmost deference for their Sex; and they fully believe that the Chief Circle Himself is not more devoutly adored by us than they are: but behind their backs they are both regarded and spoken of—by all except the very young—as being little better than "mindless organisms."

Our Theology also in the Women's chambers is entirely different from our Theology elsewhere.

Now my humble fear is that this double training, in language as well as in thought, imposes somewhat too heavy a burden upon the young, especially when, at the age of three years old, they are taken from the maternal care and taught to unlearn the old language— except for the purpose of repeating it in the presence of their Mothers and Nurses—and to learn the vocabulary and idiom of science. Already methinks I discern a weakness in the grasp of mathematical truth at the present time as compared with the more robust intellect of our ancestors three hundred years ago. I say nothing of the possible danger if a Woman should ever surreptitiously learn to read and convey to her Sex the result of her perusal of a single popular volume; nor of the possibility that the indiscretion or disobedience of some infant Male might reveal to a Mother the secrets of the logical dialect. On the simple ground of the enfeebling of the Male intellect, I rest this humble appeal to the highest Authorities to reconsider the regulations of Female education.

PART II

OTHER WORLDS

"O brave new worlds, that have such people in them!"

13.—How I had a Vision of Lineland

It was the last day but one of the 1999th year of our era, and the first day of the Long Vacation. Having amused myself till a late hour with my favourite recreation of Geometry, I had retired to rest with an unsolved problem in my mind. In the night I had a dream.

I saw before me a vast multitude of small Straight Lines (which I naturally assumed to be Women) interspersed with other Beings still smaller and of the nature of lustrous points—all moving to and fro in one and the same Straight Line, and, as nearly as I could judge, with the same velocity.

A noise of confused, multitudinous chirping or twittering issued from them at intervals as long as they were moving; but sometimes they ceased from motion, and then all was silence.

Approaching one of the largest of what I thought to be Women, I accosted her, but received no answer. A second and a third appeal on my part were equally ineffectual. Losing patience at what appeared to me intolerable rudeness, I brought my mouth into a position full in front of her mouth so as to intercept her motion, and loudly repeated my question, "Woman, what signifies this concourse, and this strange and confused chirping, and this monotonous motion to and fro in one and the same Straight Line?"

My view of Lineland

My eye • | My-self |

Women
A boy Men Men ← — — — — → The KING ← Men   men → A boy Women

The KING'S eyes

much larger than the reality

shewing that HIS MAJESTY

could see nothing but a point.

"I am no Woman," replied the small Line. "I am the Monarch of the world. But thou, whence intrudest thou into my realm of Lineland?" Receiving this abrupt reply, I begged pardon if I had in any way startled or molested his Royal Highness; and describing myself as a stranger I besought the King to give me some account of his dominions. But I had the greatest possible difficulty in obtaining any information on points that really interested me; for the Monarch could not refrain from constantly assuming that whatever was familiar to him must also be known to me and that I was simulating ignorance in jest. However, by persevering questions I elicited the following facts:

It seemed that this poor ignorant Monarch—as he called himself—was persuaded that the Straight Line which he called his Kingdom, and in which he passed his existence, constituted the whole of the world, and indeed the whole of Space. Not being able either to move or to see, save in his Straight Line, he had no conception of anything out of it. Though he had heard my voice when I first addressed him, the sounds had come to him in a manner so contrary to his experience that he had made no answer, "seeing no man," as he expressed it, "and hearing a voice as it were from my own intestines." Until the moment when I placed my mouth in his World, he had neither seen me, nor heard anything except confused sounds beating against—what I called his side, but what he called his *inside* or *stomach;* nor had he even now the least conception of the region from which I had come. Outside his World, or Line, all was a blank to him; nay, not even a blank, for a blank implies Space; say, rather, all was non-existent.

His subjects—of whom the small Lines were men and the Points Women—were all alike confined in motion and eye-sight to that single Straight Line, which was their World. It need scarcely be added that the whole of their horizon was limited to a Point; nor could any one ever see anything but a Point. Man, woman, child, thing—each was a Point to the eye of a Linelander. Only by the sound of the voice could sex or age be distinguished. Moreover, as each individual occupied the whole of the narrow path, so to speak, which constituted his Universe, and no one could move to the right or left to make way for passers by, it followed that no Linelander could ever pass another. Once neighbours, always neighbours. Neighbourhood with them was like marriage with us. Neighbours remained neighbours till death did them part.

Such a life, with all vision limited to a Point, and all motion to a Straight Line, seemed to me inexpressibly dreary; and I was surprised to note the vivacity and cheerfulness of the King. Wondering whether it was possible, amid circumstances so unfavourable to domestic relations, to enjoy the pleasures of conjugal union. I hesitated for some time to question his Royal Highness on so delicate a subject; but at last I plunged into it by abruptly inquiring as to the health of his family. "My wives and children," he replied, "are well and happy."

Staggered at this answer—for in the immediate proximity of the Monarch (as I had noted in my dream before I entered Lineland) there were none but Men—I ventured to reply, "Pardon me, but I cannot imagine how your Royal Highness can at any time either see or approach their Majesties, when there are at least half a dozen intervening individuals, whom you can neither see through, nor pass by? Is it possible that in Lineland proximity is not necessary for marriage and for the generation of children?"

"How can you ask so absurd a question?" replied the Monarch. "If it were indeed as you suggest, the Universe would soon be depopulated. No, no; neighbourhood is needless for the union of hearts; and the birth of children is too important a matter to have been allowed to depend upon such an accident as proximity. You cannot be ignorant of this. Yet since you are pleased to affect ignorance, I will instruct you as if you were the veriest baby in Lineland. Know, then, that marriages are consummated by means of the faculty of sound and the sense of hearing.

"You are of course aware that every Man has two mouths or voices—as well as two eyes—a bass at one and a tenor at the other of his extremities. I should not mention this, but that I have been unable to distinguish your tenor in the course of our conversation." I replied that I had but one voice, and that I had not been aware that his Royal Highness had two. "That confirms my impression," said the King, "that you are not a Man, but a feminine Monstrosity with a bass voice, and an utterly uneducated ear. But to continue.

"Nature having herself ordained that every Man should wed two wives—" "Why two?" asked I. "You carry your affected simplicity too far," he cried. "How can there be a completely harmonious union without the combination of the Four in One, viz. the Bass and Tenor of the Man and the Soprano and Contralto of the two Women?" "But supposing," said I, "that a man should prefer one wife or three?" "It is impossible," he said; "it is as inconceivable as that two and one should make five, or that the human eye should see a Straight Line." I would have interrupted him; but he proceeded as follows:

"Once in the middle of each week a Law of Nature compels us to move to and fro with a rhythmic motion of more than usual violence, which continues for the time you would take to count a hundred and one. In the midst of this choral dance, at the fifty-first pulsation, the inhabitants of the Universe pause in full career, and each individual sends forth his richest, fullest, sweetest strain. It is in this decisive moment that all our marriages are made. So exquisite is the adaptation of Bass to Treble, of Tenor to Contralto, that oftentimes the Loved Ones, though twenty thousand leagues away, recognize at once the responsive note of their destined Lover; and, penetrating the paltry obstacles of distance, Love unites the three. The marriage in that instant consummated results in a threefold Male and Female offspring which takes its place in Lineland."

"What! Always threefold?" said I. "Must one wife then always have twins?"

"Bass-voiced Monstrosity! yes," replied the King. "How else could the balance of the Sexes be maintained, if two girls were not born for every boy? Would you ignore the very Alphabet of Nature?" He ceased, speechless for fury; and some time elapsed before I could induce him to resume his narrative.

"You will not, of course, suppose that every bachelor among us finds his mates at the first wooing in this universal Marriage Chorus. On the contrary, the process is by most of us many times repeated. Few are the hearts whose happy lot it is at once to recognize in each other's voices the partner intended for them by Providence, and to fly into a reciprocal and perfectly harmonious embrace. With most of us the courtship is of long duration. The Wooer's voices may perhaps accord with one of the future wives, but not with both; or not, at first, with either; or the Soprano and Contralto may not quite harmonize. In such cases Nature has provided that every weekly Chorus shall bring the three Lovers into closer harmony. Each trial of voice, each fresh discovery of discord, almost imperceptibly induces the less perfect to modify his or her vocal utterance so as to approximate to the more perfect. And after many trials and many approximations, the result is at last achieved. There comes a day at last, when, while the wonted Marriage Chorus goes forth from universal Lineland, the three far-off Lovers suddenly find themselves in exact harmony, and, before they are awake, the wedded Triplet is rapt vocally into a duplicate embrace; and Nature rejoices over one more marriage and over three more births."

14.—How I vainly tried to explain the nature of Flatland

Thinking that it was time to bring down the Monarch from his raptures to the level of common sense, I determined to endeavour to open up to him some glimpses of the truth, that is to say of the nature of things in Flatland. So I began thus: "How does your Royal Highness distinguish the shapes and positions of his subjects? I for my part noticed by the sense of sight, before I entered your Kingdom, that some of your people are Lines and others Points, and that some of the Lines are larger—" "You speak of an impossibility," interrupted the King; "you must have seen a vision; for to detect the difference between a Line and a Point by the sense of sight is, as every one knows, in the nature of things, impossible; but it can be detected by the sense of hearing, and by the same means my shape can be exactly ascertained. Behold me—I am a Line, the longest in Lineland, over six inches of Space—" "Of Length," I ventured to suggest. "Fool," said he, "Space is Length. Interrupt me again, and I have done."

I apologized; but he continued scornfully, "Since you are impervious to argument, you shall hear with your ears how by means of my two voices I reveal my shape to my Wives, who are at this moment six thousand miles seventy yards two feet eight inches away, the one to the North, the other to the South. Listen, I call to them."

He chirruped, and then complacently continued: "My wives at this moment receiving the sound of one of my voices, closely followed by the other, and perceiving that the latter reaches them after an interval in which sound can traverse 6.457 inches, infer that one of my mouths is 6.457 inches further from them than the other, and accordingly know my shape to be 6.457 inches. But you will of course understand that my wives do not make this calculation every time they hear my two voices. They made it, once for all, before we were married. But they *could* make it at any time. And in the same way I can estimate the shape of any of my Male subjects by the sense of sound."

"But how," said I, "if a Man feigns a Woman's voice with one of his two voices, or so disguises his Southern voice that it cannot be recognized as the echo of the Northern? May not such deceptions cause great inconvenience? And have you no means of checking frauds of this kind by commanding your neighbouring subjects to feel one another?" This of course was a very stupid question, for feeling could not have answered the purpose; but I asked with the view of irritating the Monarch, and I succeeded perfectly.

"What!" cried he in horror, "explain your meaning." "Feel, touch, come into contact," I replied. "If you mean by *feeling*," said the King, "approaching so close as to leave no space between two individuals, know, Stranger, that this offence is punishable in my dominions by death. And the reason is obvious. The frail form of a Woman, being liable to be shattered by such an approximation, must be preserved by the State; but since Women cannot be distinguished by the sense of sight from Men, the Law ordains universally that neither Man nor Woman shall be approached so closely as to destroy the interval between the approximator and the approximated.

"And indeed what possible purpose would be served by this illegal and unnatural excess of approximation which you call *touching*, when all the ends of so brutal and coarse a process are attained at once more easily and more exactly by the sense of hearing? As to your suggested danger of deception, it is non-existent: for the Voice, being the essence of one's Being, cannot be thus changed at will. But come, suppose that I had the power of passing through solid things, so that I could penetrate my subjects, one after another, even to the number of a billion, verifying the size and distance of each by the sense of *feeling*: how much time and energy would be wasted in this clumsy and inaccurate method! Whereas now, in one moment of audition, I take as it were the census and statistics, local, corporeal, mental and spiritual, of every living being in Lineland. Hark, only hark!"

So saying he paused and listened, as if in an ecstasy, to a sound which seemed to me no better than a tiny chirping from an innumerable multitude of lilliputian grasshoppers.

"Truly," replied I, "your sense of hearing serves you in good stead, and fills up many of your deficiencies. But permit me to point out that your life in Lineland must be deplorably dull. To see nothing but a Point! Not even to be able to contemplate a Straight Line! Nay, not even to know what a Straight Line is! To see, yet be cut off from those Linear prospects which are vouchsafed to us in Flatland! Better surely to have no sense of sight at all than to see so little! I grant you I have not your discriminative faculty of hearing; for the concert of all Lineland which gives you such intense pleasure, is to me no better than a multitudinous twittering or chirping. But at least I can discern, by sight, a Line from a Point. And let me prove it. Just before I came into your kingdom, I saw you dancing from left to right, and then from right to left, with Seven Men and a Woman in your immediate proximity on the left, and eight Men and two Women on your right. Is not this correct?"

"It is correct," said the King, "so far as the numbers and sexes are concerned, though I know not what you mean by 'right' and 'left.' But I deny that you saw these things. For how could you see the Line, that is to say the inside, of any Man? But you must have heard these things, and then dreamed that you saw them. And let me ask what you mean by those words 'left' and 'right.' I suppose it is your way of saying Northward and Southward."

"Not so," replied I; "besides your motion of Northward and Southward, there is another motion which I call from right to left."

King. Exhibit to me, if you please, this motion from left to right.

I. Nay, that I cannot do, unless you could step out of your Line altogether.

King. Out of my Line? Do you mean out of the world? Out of Space?

I. Well, yes. Out of *your* World. Out of *your* Space. For your Space is not the true Space. True Space is a Plane; but your Space is only a Line.

King. If you cannot indicate this motion from left to right by yourself moving in it, then I beg you to describe it to me in words.

I. If you cannot tell your right side from your left, I fear that no words of mine can make my meaning clear to you. But surely you cannot be ignorant of so simple a distinction.

King. I do not in the least understand you.

I. Alas! How shall I make it clear? When you move straight on, does it not sometimes occur to you that you *could* move in some other way, turning your eye round so as to look in the direction towards which your side is now fronting? In other words, instead of always moving in the direction of one of your extremities, do you never feel a desire to move in the direction, so to speak, of your side?

King. Never. And what do you mean? How can a man's inside "front" in any direction? Or how can a man move in the direction of his inside?

I. Well then, since words cannot explain the matter, I will try deeds, and will move gradually out of Lineland in the direction which I desire to indicate to you.

At the word I began to move my body out of Lineland. As long as any part of me remained in his dominion and in his view, the King kept exclaiming, "I see you, I see you still; you are not moving." But when I had at last moved myself out of his Line, he cried in his shrillest voice, "She is vanished; she is dead." "I am not dead," replied I; "I am simply out of Lineland, that is to say, out of the Straight Line which you call Space, and in the true Space, where I can see things as they are. And at this moment I can see your Line, or side—or inside as you are pleased to call it; and I can see also the Men and Women on the North and South of you, whom I will now enumerate, describing their order, their size, and the interval between each."

When I had done this at great length, I cried triumphantly, "Does that at last convince you?" And, with that, I once more entered Lineland, taking up the same position as before.

But the Monarch replied, "If you were a Man of sense—though, as you appear to have only one voice I have little doubt you are not a Man but a Woman—but, if you had a particle of sense, you would listen to reason. You ask me to believe that there is another Line besides that which my senses indicate, and another motion besides that of which I am daily conscious. I, in return, ask you to describe in words or indicate by motion that other Line of which you speak. Instead of moving, you merely exercise some magic art of vanishing and returning to sight; and instead of any lucid description of your new World, you simply tell me the numbers and sizes of some forty of my retinue, facts known to any child in my capital. Can anything be more irrational or audacious? Acknowledge your folly or depart from my dominions."

Furious at his perversity, and especially indignant that he professed to be ignorant of my sex, I retorted in no measured terms, "Besotted Being! You think yourself the perfection of existence, while you are in reality the most imperfect and imbecile. You profess to see, whereas you can see nothing but a Point! You plume yourself on inferring the existence of a Straight Line; but I *can see* Straight Lines, and infer the existence of Angles, Triangles, Squares, Pentagons, Hexagons, and even Circles. Why waste more words?

Suffice it that I am the completion of your incomplete self. You are a Line, but I am a Line of Lines, called in my country a Square: and even I, infinitely superior though I am to you, am of little account among the great nobles of Flatland, whence I have come to visit you, in the hope of enlightening your ignorance."

Hearing these words the King advanced towards me with a menacing cry as if to pierce me through the diagonal; and in that same moment there arose from myriads of his subjects a multitudinous war-cry, increasing in vehemence till at last methought it rivalled the roar of an army of a hundred thousand Isosceles, and the artillery of a thousand Pentagons. Spell-bound and motionless, I could neither speak nor move to avert the impending destruction; and still the noise grew louder, and the King came closer, when I awoke to find the breakfast-bell recalling me to the realities of Flatland.

15.—Concerning a Stranger from Spaceland

From dreams I proceed to facts.

It was the last day of the 1999th year of our era. The pattering of the rain had long ago announced nightfall; and I was sitting[1] in the company of my wife, musing on the events of the past and the prospects of the coming year, the coming century, the coming Millennium.

My four Sons and two orphan Grandchildren had retired to their several apartments; and my wife alone remained with me to see the old Millennium out and the new one in.

I was rapt in thought, pondering in my mind some words that had casually issued from the mouth of my youngest Grandson, a most promising young Hexagon of unusual brilliancy and perfect angularity. His uncles and I had been giving him his usual practical lesson in Sight Recognition, turning ourselves upon

[1]When I say "sitting," of course I do not mean any change of attitude such as you in Spaceland signify by that word; for as we have no feet, we can no more "sit" nor "stand" (in your sense of the word) than one of your soles or flounders.

Nevertheless, we perfectly well recognize the different mental states of volition implied in "lying," "sitting," and "standing," which are to some extent indicated to a beholder by a slight increase of lustre corresponding to the increase of volition.

But on this, and a thousand other kindred subjects, time forbids me to dwell.

our centres, now rapidly, now more slowly, and questioning him as to our positions; and his answers had been so satisfactory that I had been induced to reward him by giving him a few hints on Arithmetic, as applied to Geometry.

Taking nine Squares, each an inch every way, I had put them together so as to make one large Square, with a side of three inches, and I had hence proved to my little Grandson that—though it was impossible for us to *see* the inside of the Square—yet we might ascertain the number of square inches in a Square by simply squaring the number of inches in the side: "and thus," said I, "we know that 3^2, or 9, represents the number of square inches in a Square whose side is 3 inches long."

The little Hexagon meditated on this a while and then said to me; "But you have been teaching me to raise numbers to the third power: I suppose 3^3 must mean something in Geometry; what does it mean?" "Nothing at all," replied I, "not at least in Geometry; for Geometry has only Two Dimensions." And then I began to shew the boy how a Point by moving through a length of three inches makes a Line of three inches, which may be represented by 3; and how a Line of three inches, moving parallel to itself through a length of three inches, makes a Square of three inches every way, which may be represented by 3^2.

Upon this, my Grandson, again returning to his former suggestion, took me up rather suddenly and exclaimed, "Well, then, if a Point by moving three inches, makes a Line of three inches represented by 3; and if a straight Line of three inches, moving parallel to itself, makes a Square of three inches every way, represented by 3^2; it must be that a Square of three inches every way, moving somehow parallel to itself (but I don't see how) must make

Something else (but I don't see what) of three inches every way—and this must be represented by 3^3."

"Go to bed," said I, a little ruffled by this interruption: "if you would talk less nonsense, you would remember more sense."

So my Grandson had disappeared in disgrace; and there I sat by my Wife's side, endeavouring to form a retrospect of the year 1999 and of the possibilities of the year 2000, but not quite able to shake off the thoughts suggested by the prattle of my bright little Hexagon. Only a few sands now remained in the half-hour glass. Rousing myself from my reverie I turned the glass Northward for the last time in the old Millennium; and in the act, I exclaimed aloud. "The boy is a fool."

Straightway I became conscious of a Presence in the room, and a chilling breath thrilled through my very being. "He is no such thing," cried my Wife, "and you are breaking the Commandments in thus dishonouring your own Grandson." But I took no notice of her. Looking round in every direction I could see nothing; yet still I *felt* a Presence, and shivered as the cold whisper came again. I started up. "What is the matter?" said my Wife, "there is no draught; what are you looking for? There is nothing." There was nothing; and I resumed my seat, again exclaiming, "The boy is a fool, I say; 3^3 can have no meaning in Geometry." At once there came a distinctly audible reply, "The boy is not a fool; and 3^3 has an obvious Geometrical meaning."

My Wife as well as myself heard the words, although she did not understand their meaning, and both of us sprang forward in the direction of the sound. What was our horror when we saw before us a Figure! At the first glance it appeared to be a Woman, seen sideways; but a moment's observation

shewed me that the extremities passed into dimness
too rapidly to represent one of the Female Sex; and I
should have thought it a Circle, only that it seemed
to change its size in a manner impossible for a Circle
or for any regular Figure of which I had had experience.

But my Wife had not my experience, nor the
coolness necessary to note these characteristics. With
the usual hastiness and unreasoning jealousy of her
Sex, she flew at once to the conclusion that a Woman
had entered the house through some small aperture.
"How comes this person here?" she exclaimed, "you
promised me, my dear, that there should be no
ventilators in our new house." "Nor are there any,"
said I; "but what makes you think that the stranger is a
Woman? I see by my power of Sight Recognition——"
"Oh, I have no patience with your Sight Recognition,"
replied she, " 'Feeling is believing' and 'A Straight
Line to the touch is worth a Circle to the sight' "—
two Proverbs, very common with the Frailer Sex
in Flatland.

"Well," said I, for I was afraid of irritating her, "if
it must be so, demand an introduction." Assuming
her most gracious manner, my Wife advanced towards
the Stranger, "Permit me, Madam, to feel and be
felt by——" then, suddenly recoiling. "Oh! it is not
a Woman, and there are no angles either, not a trace
of one. Can it be that I have so misbehaved to a
perfect Circle?"

"I am indeed, in a certain sense a Circle," replied
the Voice, "and a more perfect Circle than any in
Flatland; but to speak more accurately, I am many
Circles in one." Then he added more mildly, "I have
a message, dear Madam, to your husband, which I
must not deliver in your presence; and, if you would
suffer us to retire for a few minutes——" But my Wife
would not listen to the proposal that our august

Visitor should so incommode himself, and assuring the Circle that the hour of her own retirement had long passed, with many reiterated apologies for her recent indiscretion, she at last retreated to her apartment.

I glanced at the half-hour glass. The last sands had fallen. The third Millennium had begun.

16.—How the Stranger vainly endeavoured to reveal to me in words the mysteries of Spaceland

As soon as the sound of the Peace-cry of my departing Wife had died away, I began to approach the Stranger with the intention of taking a nearer view and of bidding him be seated: but his appearance struck me dumb and motionless with astonishment. Without the slightest symptoms of angularity he nevertheless varied every instant with gradations of size and brightness scarcely possible for any Figure within the scope of my experience. The thought flashed across me that I might have before me a burglar or cut-throat, some monstrous Irregular Isosceles, who, by feigning the voice of a Circle, had obtained admission somehow into the house, and was now preparing to stab me with his acute angle.

In a sitting-room, the absence of Fog (and the season happened to be remarkably dry), made it difficult for me to trust to Sight Recognition, especially at the short distance at which I was standing. Desperate with fear, I rushed forward with an unceremonious, "You must permit me, Sir—" and felt him. My Wife was right. There was not the trace of an angle, not the slightest roughness or inequality: never in my life had I met with a more perfect Circle. He remained motionless while I walked round him, beginning from his eye and returning to it again. Circular he was throughout, a perfectly satisfactory Circle; there could not be a doubt of it. Then followed a dialogue, which I will endeavour to set down as near as I can recollect it, omitting only some of my profuse apologies—for I was covered with shame and humiliation that I, a Square, should have been guilty of the impertinence of feeling a Circle. It was commenced by the Stranger with some impatience at the lengthiness of my introductory process.

Stranger. Have you felt me enough by this time? Are you not introduced to me yet?

I. Most illustrious Sir, excuse my awkwardness, which arises not from ignorance of the usages of polite society, but from a little surprise and nervousness, consequent on this somewhat unexpected visit. And I beseech you to reveal my indiscretion to no one, and especially not to my Wife. But before your Lordship enters into further communications, would he deign to satisfy the curiosity of one who would gladly know whence his Visitor came?

Stranger. From Space, from Space, Sir: whence else?

I. Pardon me, my Lord, but is not your Lordship already in Space, your Lordship and his humble servant, even at this moment?

Stranger. Pooh! what do you know of Space? Define Space.

I. Space, my Lord, is height and breadth indefinitely prolonged.

Stranger. Exactly: you see you do not even know what Space is. You think it is of Two Dimensions only; but I have come to announce to you a Third—height, breadth, and length.

I. Your Lordship is pleased to be merry. We also speak of length and height, or breadth and thickness, thus denoting Two Dimensions by four names.

Stranger. But I mean not only three names, but Three Dimensions.

I. Would your Lordship indicate or explain to me in what direction is the Third Dimension, unknown to me?

Stranger. I came from it. It is up above and down below.

I. My Lord means seemingly that it is Northward and Southward.

Stranger. I mean nothing of the kind. I mean a direction in which you cannot look, because you have no eye in your side.

I. Pardon me, my Lord, a moment's inspection will convince your Lordship that I have a perfect-luminary at the juncture of two of my sides.

Stranger. Yes: but in order to see into Space you ought to have an eye, not on your Perimeter, but on your side, that is, on what you would probably call your inside; but we in Spaceland should call it your side.

I. An eye in my inside! An eye in my stomach! Your Lordship jests.

Stranger. I am in no jesting humour. I tell you that I come from Space, or, since you will not understand what Space means, from the Land of Three Dimensions whence I but lately looked down upon your Plane which you call Space forsooth. From that position of advantage I discerned all that you speak of as *solid* (by which you mean "enclosed on four sides"), your houses, your churches, your very chests and safes, yes even your insides and stomachs, all lying open and exposed to my view.

I. Such assertions are easily made, my Lord.

Stranger. But not easily proved, you mean. But I mean to prove mine.

When I descended here, I saw your four Sons, the

Pentagons, each in his apartment, and your two Grandsons the Hexagons; I saw your youngest Hexagon
remain a while with you and then retire to his room,
leaving you and your Wife alone. I saw your Isosceles servants, three in number, in the kitchen at
supper, and the little Page in the scullery. Then I
came here, and how do you think I came?

I. Through the roof, I suppose.

Stranger. Not so. Your roof, as you know very
well, has been recently repaired, and has no aperture by which even a Woman could penetrate. I tell
you I come from Space. Are you not convinced by
what I have told you of your children and household?

I. Your Lordship must be aware that such facts
touching the belongings of his humble servant might
be easily ascertained by any one in the neighbourhood
possessing your Lordship's ample means of obtaining
information.

Stranger. (*To himself.*) What must I do? Stay; one
more argument suggests itself to me. When you see
a Straight Line—your wife, for example—how many
Dimensions do you attribute to her?

I. Your Lordship would treat me as if I were one
of the vulgar who, being ignorant of Mathematics,
suppose that a Woman is really a Straight Line, and
only of One Dimension. No, no, my Lord; we Squares
are better advised, and are as well aware as your
Lordship that a Woman, though popularly called a
Straight Line, is, really and scientifically, a very thin
Parallelogram, possessing Two Dimensions, like the
rest of us, viz., length and breadth (or thickness).

Stranger. But the very fact that a Line is visible
implies that it possesses yet another Dimension.

I. My Lord, I have just acknowledged that a Woman
is broad as well as long. We see her length, we infer

her breadth; which, though very slight, is capable of measurement.

Stranger. You do not understand me. I mean that when you see a Woman, you ought—besides inferring her breadth—to see her length, and to *see* what we call her *height*; although that last Dimension is infinitesimal in your country. If a Line were mere length without "height," it would cease to occupy Space and would become invisible. Surely you must recognize this?

I. I must indeed confess that I do not in the least understand your Lordship. When we in Flatland see a Line, we see length and *brightness*. If the brightness disappears, the Line is extinguished, and, as you say, ceases to occupy Space. But am I to suppose that your Lordship gives to brightness the title of a Dimension, and that what we call "bright" you call "high"?

Stranger. No, indeed. By "height" I mean a Dimension like your length: only, with you, "height" is not so easily perceptible, being extremely small.

I. My Lord, your assertion is easily put to the test. You say I have a Third Dimension, which you call "height." Now, Dimension implies direction and measurement. Do but measure my "height" or merely indicate to me the direction in which my "height" extends, and I will become your convert. Otherwise, your Lordship's own understanding must hold me excused.

Stranger. (*To himself*.) I can do neither. How shall I convince him? Surely a plain statement of facts followed by ocular demonstration ought to suffice. —Now, Sir; listen to me.

You are living on a Plane. What you style Flatland is the vast level surface of what I may call a fluid, on, or in, the top of which you and your countrymen move about, without rising above it or falling below it.

I am not a plane Figure, but a Solid. You call me a Circle; but in reality I am not a Circle, but an infinite number of Circles, of size varying from a Point to a Circle of thirteen inches in diameter, one placed on the top of the other. When I cut through your plane as I am now doing, I make in your plane a section which you, very rightly, call a Circle. For even a Sphere—which is my proper name in my own country—if he manifest himself at all to an inhabitant of Flatland—must needs manifest himself as a Circle.

Do you not remember—for I, who see all things, discerned last night the phantasmal vision of Lineland written upon your brain—do you not remember, I say, how, when you entered the realm of Lineland, you were compelled to manifest yourself to the King, not as a Square, but as a Line, because that Linear Realm had not Dimensions enough to represent the whole of you, but only a slice or section of you? In precisely the same way, your country of Two Dimensions is not spacious enough to represent me, a being of Three, but can only exhibit a slice or section of me, which is what you call a Circle.

The diminished brightness of your eye indicates incredulity. But now prepare to receive proof positive of the truth of my assertions. You cannot indeed see more than one of my sections, or Circles, at a time; for you have no power to raise your eye out of the plane of Flatland; but you can at least see that, as I rise in Space, so my sections become smaller. See now, I will rise; and the effect upon your eye will be that my Circle will become smaller and smaller till it dwindles to a point and finally vanishes.

There was no "rising" that I could see; but he diminished and finally vanished. I winked once or twice to make sure that I was not dreaming. But it was no dream. For from the depths of nowhere came forth a hollow voice—close to my heart is seemed—"Am I quite gone? Are you convinced now? Well, now I will gradually return to Flatland and you shall see my section become larger and larger."

Every reader in Spaceland will easily understand that my mysterious Guest was speaking the language of truth and even of simplicity. But to me, proficient though I was in Flatland Mathematics, it was by no means a simple matter. The rough diagram given above will make it clear to any Spaceland child that the Sphere, ascending in the three positions indicated there, must needs have manifested himself to me, or to any Flatlander, as a Circle, at first of full size, then small, and at last very small indeed, approaching to a Point. But to me, although I saw the facts before me, the causes were as dark as ever. All that I could comprehend was, that the Circle had made himself smaller and vanished, and that he had now reappeared and was rapidly making himself larger.

When he regained his original size, he heaved a deep sigh; for he perceived by my silence that I had altogether failed to comprehend him. And indeed I was now inclining to the belief that he must be no Circle at all, but some extremely clever juggler; or else that the old wives' tales were true, and that after all there were such people as Enchanters and Magicians.·

After a long pause he muttered to himself, "One resource alone remains, if I am not to resort to action, I must try the method of Analogy." Then followed a still longer silence, after which he continued our dialogue.

Sphere. Tell me, Mr. Mathematician; if a Point moves Northward, and leaves a luminous wake, what name would you give to the wake?

I. A straight Line.

Sphere. And a straight Line has how many extremities?

I. Two.

Sphere. Now conceive the Northward straight Line moving parallel to itself, East and West, so that every point in it leaves behind it the wake of a straight Line. What name will you give to the Figure thereby formed? We will suppose that it moves through a distance equal to the original straight Line. —What name, I say?

I. A Square.

Sphere. And how many sides has a Square? How many angles?

I. Four sides and four angles.

Sphere. Now stretch your imagination a little, and conceive a Square in Flatland, moving parallel to itself upward.

I. What? Northward?

Sphere. No, not Northward; upward; out of Flatland altogether.

If it moved Northward, the Southern points in the Square would have to move through the positions previously occupied by the Northern points. But that is not my meaning.

I mean that every Point in you—for you are a

Square and will serve the purpose of my illustration—
every Point in you, that is to say in what you call
your inside, is to pass upwards through Space in
such a way that no Point shall pass through the
position previously occupied by any other Point; but
each Point shall describe a straight Line of its own.
This is all in accordance with Analogy; surely it must
be clear to you.

Restraining my impatience—for I was now under a
strong temptation to rush blindly at my Visitor and
to precipitate him into Space, or out of Flatland,
anywhere, so that I could get rid of him—I replied:—

"And what may be the nature of the Figure which
I am to shape out by this motion which you are
pleased to denote by the word 'upward'? I presume
it is describable in the language of Flatland."

Sphere. Oh, certainly. It is all plain and simple,
and in strict accordance with Analogy—only, by the
way, you must not speak of the result as being a
Figure, but as a Solid. But I will describe it to you.
Or rather not I, but Analogy.

We began with a single Point, which of course—
being itself a Point—has only *one* terminal Point.

One Point produces a Line with *two* terminal Points.

One Line produces a Square with *four* terminal
Points.

Now you can give yourself the answer to your own
question: 1, 2, 4, are evidently in Geometrical
Progression. What is the next number?

I. Eight.

Sphere. Exactly. The one Square produces a
*Something-which-you-do-not-as-yet-know-a-name-for-
but-which-we-call-a-Cube* with *eight* terminal Points.
Now are you convinced?

I. And has this Creature sides, as well as angles or
what you call "terminal Points"?

Sphere. Of course; and all according to Analogy. But, by the way, not what *you* call sides, but what *we* call sides. You would call them *solids.*

I. And how many solids or sides will appertain to this Being whom I am to generate by the motion of my inside in an "upward" direction, and whom you call a Cube?

Sphere. How can you ask? And you a mathematician! The side of anything is always, if I may so say, one Dimension behind the thing. Consequently, as there is no Dimension behind a Point, a Point has 0 sides; a Line, if I may say, has 2 sides (for the Points of a Line may be called by courtesy, its sides); a Square has 4 sides; 0, 2, 4; what Progression do you call that?

I. Arithmetical.

Sphere. And what is the next number?

I. Six.

Sphere. Exactly. Then you see you have answered your own question. The Cube which you will generate will be bounded by six sides, that is to say, six of your insides. You see it all now, eh?

"Monster," I shrieked, "be thou juggler, enchanter, dream, or devil, no more will I endure thy mockeries. Either thou or I must perish." And saying these words I precipitated myself upon him.

17.—How the Sphere, having in vain tried words, resorted to deeds

It was in vain. I brought my hardest right angle into violent collision with the Stranger, pressing on him with a force sufficient to have destroyed any ordinary Circle: but I could feel him slowly and unarrestably slipping from my contact; no edging to the right nor to the left, but moving somehow out of the world, and vanishing to nothing. Soon there was a blank. But still I heard the Intruder's voice.

Sphere. Why will you refuse to listen to reason? I had hoped to find in you—as being a man of sense and an accomplished mathematician—a fit apostle for the Gospel of the Three Dimensions, which I am allowed to preach once only in a thousand years: but now I know not how to convince you. Stay, I have it. Deeds, and not words, shall proclaim the truth. Listen, my friend.

I have told you I can see from my position in Space the inside of all things that you consider closed. For example, I see in yonder cupboard near which you are standing, several of what you call boxes (but like everything else in Flatland, they have no tops nor bottoms) full of money; I see also two tablets of accounts. I am about to descend into that cupboard and to bring you one of those tablets. I saw you lock the cupboard half an hour ago, and I know you have the key in your possession. But I descend from Space;

the doors, you see, remain unmoved. Now I am in the cupboard and am taking the tablet. Now I have it. Now I ascend with it.

I rushed to the closet and dashed the door open. One of the tablets was gone. With a mocking laugh, the Stranger appeared in the other corner of the room, and at the same time the tablet appeared upon the floor. I took it up. There could be no doubt—it was the missing tablet.

I groaned with horror, doubting whether I was not out of my senses; but the Stranger continued: "Surely you must now see that my explanation, and no other, suits the phenomena. What you call Solid things are really superficial; what you call Space is really nothing but a great Plane. I am in Space, and look down upon the insides of the things of which you only see the outsides. You could leave this Plane yourself, if you could but summon up the necessary volition. A slight upward or downward motion would enable you to see all that I can see.

"The higher I mount, and the further I go from your Plane, the more I can see, though of course I see it on a smaller scale. For example, I am ascending; now I can see your neighbour the Hexagon and his family in their several apartments; now I see the inside of the Theatre, ten doors off, from which the audience is only just departing; and on the other side a Circle in his study, sitting at his books. Now I shall come back to you. And, as a crowning proof, what do you say to my giving you a touch, just the least touch, in your stomach? It will not seriously injure you, and the slight pain you may suffer cannot be compared with the mental benefit you will receive."

Before I could utter a word of remonstrance, I felt a shooting pain in my inside, and a demoniacal laugh seemed to issue from within me. A moment afterwards the sharp agony had ceased, leaving nothing but a dull ache behind, and the Stranger began to reappear, saying, as he gradually increased in size, "There, I have not hurt you much, have I? If you are not convinced now, I don't know what will convince you. What say you?"

My resolution was taken. It seemed intolerable that I should endure existence subject to the arbitrary visitations of a Magician who could thus play tricks with one's very stomach. If only I could in any way manage to pin him against the wall till help came!

Once more I dashed my hardest angle against him, at the same time alarming the whole household by my cries for aid. I believe, at the moment on my onset, the Stranger had sunk below our Plane, and really found difficulty in rising. In any case he remained motionless, while I, hearing, as I thought, the sound of some help approaching, pressed against him with redoubled vigour, and continued to shout for assistance.

A convulsive shudder ran through the Sphere. "This must not be," I thought I heard him say: "either he must listen to reason, or I must have recourse to the last resourse of civilization." Then, addressing me in a louder tone, he hurriedly exclaimed, "Listen: no stranger must witness what you have witnessed. Send your Wife back at once, before she enters the apartment. The Gospel of Three Dimensions must not be thus frustrated. Not thus must the fruits of one thousand years of waiting be thrown away. I hear her coming. Back! back! Away from me, or you must go with me—whither you know not—into the Land of Three Dimensions!"

"Fool! Madman! Irregular!" I exclaimed; "never

will I release thee; thou shalt pay the penalty of thine impostures."

"Ha! Is it come to this?" thundered the Stranger: "then meet your fate: out of your Plane you go. Once, twice, thrice! 'Tis done!"

18.—How I came to Spaceland, and what I saw there

An unspeakable horror seized me. There was a darkness; then a dizzy, sickening sensation of sight that was not like seeing; I saw a Line that was no Line; Space that was not Space: I was myself, and not myself. When I could find voice, I shrieked aloud in agony, "Either this is madness or it is Hell." "It is neither," calmly replied the voice of the Sphere, "it is Knowledge; it is Three Dimensions: open your eye once again and try to look steadily."

I looked, and, behold, a new world! There stood before me, visibly incorporate, all that I had before inferred, conjectured, dreamed, of perfect Circular beauty. What seemed the centre of the Stranger's form lay open to my view: yet I could see no heart, nor lungs, nor arteries, only a beautiful harmonious Something—for which I had no words; but you, my Readers in Spaceland, would call it the surface of the Sphere.

Prostrating myself mentally before my Guide, I cried, "How is it, O divine ideal of consummate loveliness and wisdom that I see thy inside, and yet cannot discern thy heart, thy lungs, thy arteries, thy liver?" "What you think you see, you see not," he replied; "it is not given to you, nor to any other Being to behold my internal parts. I am of a different order of Beings from those in Flatland. Were I a

Circle, you could discern my intestines, but I am a Being, composed as I told you before, of many Circles, the Many in the One, called in this country a Sphere. And, just as the outside of a Cube is a Square, so the outside of a Sphere presents the appearance of a Circle."

Bewildered though I was by my Teacher's enigmatic utterance, I no longer chafed against it, but worshipped him in silent adoration. He continued, with more mildness in his voice. "Distress not yourself if you cannot at first understand the deeper mysteries of Spaceland. By degrees they will dawn upon you. Let us begin by casting back a glance at the region whence you came. Return with me a while to the plains of Flatland, and I will shew you that which you have often reasoned and thought about, but never seen with the sense of sight—a visible angle." "Impossible!" I cried; but, the Sphere leading the way, I followed as if in a dream, till once more his voice arrested me: "Look yonder, and behold your own Pentagonal house, and all its inmates."

I looked below, and saw with my physical eye all that domestic individuality which I had hitherto merely inferred with the understanding. And how poor and shadowy was the inferred conjecture in comparison with the reality which I now beheld! My four Sons calmly asleep in the North-Western rooms, my two orphan Grandsons to the South; the Servants, the Butler, my Daughter, all in their several apartments. Only my affectionate Wife, alarmed by my continued absence, had quitted her room and was roving up and down in the Hall, anxiously awaiting my return. Also the Page, aroused by my cries, had left his room, and under pretext of ascertaining whether I had fallen somewhere in a faint, was prying into the cabinet in my study. All this I could now *see*, not merely infer; and as we came nearer and nearer, I could discern even the contents of my cabinet, and the two chests of gold, and the tablets of which the Sphere had made mention.

Touched by my Wife's distress, I would have sprung downward to reassure her, but I found myself incapable of motion. "Trouble not yourself about your Wife," said my Guide: "she will not be long left in anxiety; meantime, let us take a survey of Flatland."

Once more I felt myself rising through space. It was even as the Sphere had said. The further we receded from the object we beheld, the larger became the field of vision. My native city, with the interior of every house and every creature therein, lay open to my view in miniature. We mounted higher, and lo, the secrets of the earth, the depths of mines and inmost caverns of the hills, were bared before me.

Awestruck at the sight of the mysteries of the

earth, thus unveiled before my unworthy eye, I said
to my Companion, "Behold, I am become as a God.
For the wise men in our country say that to see all
things, or as they express it, *omnividence*, is the
attribute of God alone." There was something of
scorn in the voice of my Teacher as he made answer:
"Is it so indeed? Then the very pick-pockets and
cut-throats of my country are to be worshipped by
your wise men as being Gods: for there is not one of
them that does not see as much as you see now. But
trust me, your wise men are wrong."

I. Then is omnividence the attribute of others
besides Gods?

Sphere. I do not know. But, if a pick-pocket or a
cut-throat of our country can see everything that is in
your country, surely that is no reason why the pick-
pocket or cut-throat should be accepted by you as a
God. This omnividence, as you call it—it is not a
common word in Spaceland—does it make you more
just, more merciful, less selfish, more loving? Not in
the least. Then how does it make you more divine?

I. "More merciful, more loving!" But these are the
qualities of women! And we know that a Circle is a
higher Being than a Straight Line, in so far as knowledge and wisdom are more to be esteemed than
mere affection.

Sphere. It is not for me to classify human faculties
according to merit. Yet many of the best and wisest
in Spaceland think more of the affections than of the
understanding, more of your despised Straight Lines
than of your belauded Circles. But enough of this.
Look yonder. Do you know that building?

I looked, and afar off I saw an immense Polygonal
structure, in which I recognized the General Assembly Hall of the States of Flatland, surrounded by
dense lines of Pentagonal buildings at right angles to

each other, which I knew to be streets; and I perceived that I was approaching the great Metropolis.

"Here we descend," said my Guide. It was now morning, the first hour of the first day of the two thousandth year of our era. Acting, as was their wont, in strict accordance with precedent, the highest Circles of the realm were meeting in solemn conclave, as they had met on the first hour of the first day of the year 1000, and also on the first hour of the first day of the year 0.

The minutes of the previous meetings were now read by one whom I at once recognized as my brother, a perfectly Symmetrical Square, and the Chief Clerk of the High Council. It was found recorded on each occasion that: "Whereas the States had been troubled by divers ill-intentioned persons pretending to have received revelations from another World, and professing to produce demonstrations whereby they had instigated to frenzy both themselves and others, it had been for this cause unanimously resolved by the Grand Council that on the first day of each millenary, special injunctions be sent to the Prefects in the several districts of Flatland, to make strict search for such misguided persons, and without formality of mathematical examination, to destroy all such as were Isosceles of any degree, to scourge and imprison any regular Triangle, to cause any Square or Pentagon to be sent to the district Asylum, and to arrest any one of higher rank, sending him straightway to the Capital to be examined and judged by the Council."

"You hear your fate," said the Sphere to me, while the Council was passing for the third time the formal resolution. "Death or imprisonment awaits the Apostle of the Gospel of Three Dimensions." "Not so," replied I, "the matter is now so clear to me, the nature of real space so palpable, that methinks I could make a child understand it. Permit me but to descend at this moment and enlighten them." "Not yet," said my Guide, "the time will come for that. Meantime I must perform my mission. Stay thou there in thy place." Saying these words, he leaped with great dexterity into the sea (if I may so call it) of Flatland, right in the midst of the ring of Counsellors. "I come," cried he, "to proclaim that there is a land of Three Dimensions."

I could see many of the younger Counsellors start back in manifest horror, as the Sphere's circular section widened before them. But on a sign from the presiding Circle—who shewed not the slightest alarm or surprise—six Isosceles of a low type from six different quarters rushed upon the Sphere. "We have him," they cried; "No; yes; we have him still! he's going! he's gone!"

"My Lords," said the President to the Junior Circles of the Council, "there is not the slightest need for surprise; the secret archives, to which I alone have access, tell me that a similar occurrence happened on the last two millennial commencements. You will, of course, say nothing of these trifles outside the Cabinet."

Raising his voice, he now summoned the guards. "Arrest the policemen; gag them. You know your duty." After he had consigned to their fate the wretched policemen—ill-fated and unwilling witnesses of a State-secret which they were not to be permitted to reveal—he again addressed the Counsellors. "My Lords, the business of the Council being concluded, I have only to wish you a happy New Year." Before departing, he expressed, at some length, to the Clerk, my excellent but most unfortunate brother, his sincere regret that, in accordance with

precedent and for the sake of secrecy, he must condemn him to perpetual imprisonment, but added his
satisfaction that, unless some mention were made by
him of that day's incident, his life would be spared.

19.—How, though the Sphere shewed me other mysteries of Spaceland, I still desired more; and what came of it

When I saw my poor brother led away to imprisonment, I attempted to leap down into the Council Chamber, desiring to intercede on his behalf, or at least bid him farewell. But I found that I had no motion of my own. I absolutely depended on the volition of my Guide, who said in gloomy tones, "Heed not thy brother; haply thou shalt have ample time hereafter to condole with him. Follow me."

(1)   (2)

Once more we ascended into space. "Hitherto," said the Sphere, "I have shewn you naught save Plane Figures and their interiors. Now I must introduce you to Solids, and reveal to you the plan upon which they are constructed. Behold this multitude of moveable square cards. See, I put one on another, not, as you supposed, Northward of the other, but *on* the other. Now a second, now a third. See, I am building up a Solid by a multitude of Squares parallel to one another. Now t

high as it is long and br

"Pardon me, my Lord,

the appearance is as of a

inside is laid open to the

methinks I see no Solid, but

in Flatland; only of an Irregu

some monstrous criminal, so th

is painful to my eyes."

"True," said the Sphere, "it app

because you are not accustomed t

and perspective; just as in Flatland a

appear a Straight Line to one who ha

Sight Recognition. But in reality it is a

shall learn by the sense of Feeling."

He then introduced me to the Cube, a

that this marvellous Being was indeed no

a Solid; and that he was endowed with six pl

and eight terminal points called solid angle

remembered the saying of the Sphere that jus

a Creature as this would be formed by a S

moving, in Space, parallel to himself: and I rejo

to think that so insignificant a Creature as I could

some sense be called the Progenitor of so illustriou

an offspring.

But still I could not fully understand the meaning

of what my Teacher had told me concerning "light"

and "shade" and "perspective"; and I did not hesitate

to put my difficulties before him.

Were I to give the Sphere's explanation of these

matters, succinct and clear though it was, it would

be tedious to an inhabitant of Space, who knows

these things already. Suffice it, that by his lucid

statements, and by changing the position of objects

and lights, and by allowing me to feel the several

objects and even his own sacred Person, he at last

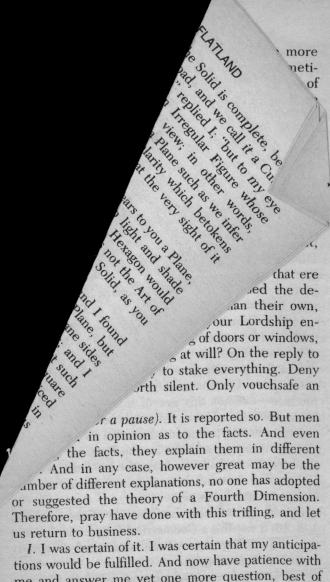

more
meti-
of

e Solid is complete, be
ad, and we call it a Cu
", replied I; "but to my eye
Irregular Figure whose
view, in other words,
a Plane such as we infer
larity which betokens
at the very sight of it
ars to you a Plane,
light and shade
Hexagon would
not the Art of
Solid, as you
nd I found
Plane, but
ane sides
and I
such
uare
ced
in

that ere
ed the de-
an their own,
our Lordship en-
of doors or windows,
at will? On the reply to
to stake everything. Deny
rth silent. Only vouchsafe an

r a pause). It is reported so. But men
in opinion as to the facts. And even
the facts, they explain them in different
And in any case, however great may be the
mber of different explanations, no one has adopted
or suggested the theory of a Fourth Dimension.
Therefore, pray have done with this trifling, and let
us return to business.

I. I was certain of it. I was certain that my anticipations would be fulfilled. And now have patience with
me and answer me yet one more question, best of
Teachers! Those who have thus appeared—no one
knows whence—and have returned—no one knows

whither—have they also contracted their sections and vanished somehow into that more Spacious Space, whither I now entreat you to conduct me?

Sphere (moodily). They have vanished, certainly—if they ever appeared. But most people say that these visions arose from the thought—you will not understand me—from the brain; from the perturbed angularity of the Seer.

I. Say they so? Oh, believe them not. Or if it indeed be so, that this other Space is really Thoughtland, then take me to that blessed Region where I in Thought shall see the insides of all solid things. There, before my ravished eye, a Cube, moving in some altogether new direction, but strictly according to Analogy, so as to make every particle of his interior pass through a new kind of Space, with a wake of its own—shall create a still more perfect perfection than himself, with sixteen terminal Extra-solid angles, and Eight solid Cubes for his Perimeter. And once there, shall we stay our upward course? In that blessed region of Four Dimensions, shall we linger on the threshold of the Fifth, and not enter therein? Ah, no! Let us rather resolve that our ambition shall soar with our corporal ascent. Then, yielding to our intellectual onset, the gates of the Sixth Dimension shall fly open; after that a Seventh, and then an Eighth—

How long I should have continued I know not. In vain did the Sphere, in his voice of thunder, reiterate his command of silence, and threaten me with the direst penalties if I persisted. Nothing could stem the flood of my ecstatic aspirations. Perhaps I was to blame; but indeed I was intoxicated with the recent draughts of Truth to which he himself had introduced me. However, the end was not long in coming. My words were cut short by a crash outside, and a simultaneous crash inside me, which impelled me through space with a velocity that precluded speech. Down! down! down! I was rapidly descending; and I knew that return to Flatland was my doom. One glimpse, one last and never-to-be-forgotten glimpse I had of that dull level wilderness—which was now to become my Universe again—spread out before my eye. Then a darkness. Then a final, all-consummating thunder-peal; and, when I came to myself, I was once more a common creeping Square, in my Study at home, listening to the Peace-Cry of my approaching Wife.

20.—How the Sphere encouraged me in a Vision

Although I had less than a minute for reflection, I felt, by a kind of instinct, that I must conceal my experiences from my Wife. Not that I apprehended, at the moment, any danger from her divulging my secret, but I knew that to any Woman in Flatland the narrative of my adventures must needs be unintelligible. So I endeavoured to reassure her by some story, invented for the occasion, that I had accidentally fallen through the trap-door of the cellar, and had there lain stunned.

The Southward attraction in our country is so slight that even to a Woman my tale necessarily appeared extraordinary and well-nigh incredible; but my Wife, whose good sense far exceeds that of the average of her Sex, and who perceived that I was unusually excited, did not argue with me on the subject, but insisted that I was ill and required repose. I was glad of an excuse for retiring to my chamber to think quietly over what had happened. When I was at last by myself, a drowsy sensation fell on me; but before my eyes closed I endeavoured to reproduce the Third Dimension, and especially the process by which a Cube is constructed through the motion of a Square. It was not so clear as I could have wished; but I remembered that it must be "Upward, and yet not Northward," and I determined steadfastly to retain these words as the clue which, if firmly grasped, could not fail to guide me to the solution. So mechanically repeating, like a charm, the words, "Upward, yet not Northward," I fell into a sound refreshing sleep.

During my slumber I had a dream. I thought I was once more by the side of the Sphere, whose lustrous hue betokened that he had exchanged his wrath against me for perfect placability. We were moving together towards a bright but infinitesimally small Point, to which my Master directed my attention. As we approached, methought there issued from it a slight humming noise as from one of your Spaceland blue-bottles, only less resonant by far, so slight indeed that even in the perfect stillness of the Vacuum through which we soared, the sound reached not our ears till we checked our flight at a distance from it of something under twenty human diagonals.

"Look yonder," said my Guide, "in Flatland thou hast lived; of Lineland thou hast received a vision; thou hast soared with me to the heights of Spaceland; now, in order to complete the range of thy experience, I conduct thee downward to the lowest depth of existence, even to the realm of Pointland, the Abyss of No dimensions.

"Behold yon miserable creature. That Point is a Being like ourselves, but confined to the non-dimensional Gulf. He is himself his own World, his own Universe; of any other than himself he can form no conception; he knows not Length, nor Breadth, nor Height, for he has had no experience of them; he has no cognizance even of the number Two; nor has he a thought of Plurality; for he is himself his One and All, being really Nothing. Yet mark his perfect self-contentment, and hence learn this lesson, that to be self-contented is to be vile and ignorant, and that to aspire is better than to be blindly and impotently happy. Now listen."

He ceased; and there arose from the little buzzing creature a tiny, low, monotonous, but distinct tinkling, as from one of your Spaceland phonographs, from which I caught these words, "Infinite beatitude of existence! It is; and there is none else beside it."

"What," said I, "does the puny creature mean by 'it'?" "He means himself," said the Sphere: "have you not noticed before now, that babies and babyish people who cannot distinguish themselves from the world, speak of themselves in the Third Person? But hush!"

"It fills all Space," continued the little soliloquizing Creature, "and what It fills, It is. What It thinks, that It utters; and what It utters, that It hears; and It itself is Thinker, Utterer, Hearer, Thought, Word, Audition; it is the One, and yet the All in All. Ah, the happiness ah, the happiness of Being!"

"Can you not startle the little thing out of its complacency?" said I. "Tell it what it really is, as you told me; reveal to it the narrow limitations of Pointland, and lead it up to something higher." "That is no easy task," said my Master; "try you."

Hereon, raising my voice to the uttermost, I addressed the Point as follows:

"Silence, silence, contemptible Creature. You call yourself the All in All, but you are the Nothing: your so-called Universe is a mere speck in a Line, and a Line is a mere shadow as compared with—" "Hush, hush, you have said enough," interrupted the Sphere, "now listen, and mark the effect of your harangue on the King of Pointland."

The lustre of the Monarch, who beamed more brightly than ever upon hearing my words, shewed clearly that he retained his complacency; and I had hardly ceased when he took up his strain again. "Ah, the joy, ah, the joy of Thought! What can It not achieve by thinking! Its own Thought coming to Itself, suggestive of Its disparagement, thereby to enhance Its happiness! Sweet rebellion stirred up to result in triumph! Ah, the divine creative power of the All in One! Ah, the joy, the joy of Being!"

"You see," said my Teacher, "how little your words have done. So far as the Monarch understands them at all, he accepts them as his own—for he cannot conceive of any other except himself—and plumes himself upon the variety of 'Its Thought' as an instance of creative Power. Let us leave this God of Pointland to the ignorant fruition of his omnipresence and omniscience: nothing that you or I can do can rescue him from his self-satisfaction."

After this, as we floated gently back to Flatland, I could hear the mild voice of my Companion pointing the moral of my vision, and stimulating me to aspire, and to teach others to aspire. He had been angered at first—he confessed—by my ambition to soar to Dimensions above the Third; but, since then, he had received fresh insight, and he was not too proud to acknowledge his error to a Pupil. Then he proceeded to initiate me into mysteries yet higher than those I had witnessed, shewing me how to construct Extra-Solids by the motion of Solids, and Double Extra-Solids by the motion of Extra-Solids, and all "strictly according to Analogy," all by methods so simple, so easy, as to be patent even to the Female Sex.

21.—How I tried to teach the Theory of Three Dimensions to my Grandson, and with what success

I awoke rejoicing, and began to reflect on the glorious career before me. I would go forth, methought, at once, and evangelize the whole of Flatland. Even to Women and Soldiers should the Gospel of Three Dimensions be proclaimed. I would begin with my Wife.

Just as I had decided on the plan of my operation, I heard the sound of many voices in the street commanding silence. Then followed a louder voice. It was a herald's proclamation. Listening attentively, I recognized the words of the Resolution of the Council, enjoining the arrest, imprisonment, or execution of any one who should pervert the minds of the people by delusions, and by professing to have received revelations from another World.

I reflected. This danger was not to be trifled with. It would be better to avoid it by omitting all mention of my Revelation, and by proceeding on the path of Demonstration—which after all, seemed so simple and so conclusive that nothing would be lost by discarding the former means. "Upward, not Northward"—was the clue to the whole proof. It had seemed to me fairly clear before I fell asleep; and when I first awoke, fresh from my dream, it had appeared as patent as Arithmetic; but somehow it did not seem to me quite so obvious now. Though my Wife entered the room opportunely just at that moment, I decided, after we had exchanged a few words of commonplace conversation, not to begin with her.

My Pentagonal Sons were men of character and standing, and physicians of no mean reputation, but not great in mathematics, and, in that respect, unfit for my purpose. But it occurred to me that a young and docile Hexagon, with a mathematical turn, would be a most suitable pupil. Why therefore not make my first experiment with my little precocious Grandson, whose casual remarks on the meaning of 3^3 had met with the approval of the Sphere? Discussing the matter with him, a mere boy, I should be in perfect safety; for he would know nothing of the Proclamation of the Council; whereas I could not feel sure that my Sons—so greatly did their patriotism and reverence for the Circles predominate over mere blind affection—might not feel compelled to hand me over to the Prefect, if they found me seriously maintaining the seditious heresy of the Third Dimension.

But the first thing to be done was to satisfy in some way the curiosity of my Wife, who naturally wished to know something of the reasons for which the Circle had desired that mysterious interview, and of the means by which he had entered the house. Without entering into the details of the elaborate account I gave her,—an account, I fear, not quite so consistent with truth as my Readers in Spaceland might desire,—I must be content with saying that I succeeded at last in persuading her to return quietly to her household duties without eliciting from me any reference to the World of Three Dimensions. This done, I immediately sent for my Grandson; for, to confess the truth, I felt that all that

I had seen and heard was in some strange way slipping away from me, like the image of a half-grasped, tantalizing dream, and I longed to essay my skill in making a first disciple.

When my Grandson entered the room I carefully secured the door. Then, sitting down by his side and taking our mathematical tablets,—or, as you would call them, Lines—I told him we would resume the lesson of yesterday. I taught him once more how a Point by motion in One Dimension produces a Line, and how a straight Line in Two Dimensions produces a Square. After this, forcing a laugh, I said, "And now, you scamp, you wanted to make me believe that a Square may in the same way by motion 'Upward, not Northward' produce another figure, a sort of extra Square in Three Dimensions. Say that again, you young rascal."

At this moment we heard once more the herald's "O yes! O yes!" outside in the street proclaiming the Resolution of the Council. Young though he was, my Grandson—who was unusually intelligent for his age, and bred up in perfect reverence for the authority of the Circles—took in the situation with an acuteness for which I was quite unprepared. He remained silent till the last words of the Proclamation had died away, and then, bursting into tears, "Dear Grandpapa," he said, "that was only my fun, and of course I meant nothing at all by it; and we did not know anything then about the new Law; and I don't think I said anything about the Third Dimension; and I am sure I did not say one word about 'Upward, not Northward,' for that would be such nonsense, you know. How could a thing move Upward, and not Northward? Upward and not Northward! Even if I were a baby, I could not be so absurd as that. How silly it is! Ha! ha! ha!"

"Not at all silly," said I, losing my temper; "here for example, I take this Square," and, at the word, I grasped a moveable Square, which was lying at hand—"and I move it, you see, not Northward but—yes, I move it Upward—that is to say, not Northward, but I move it somewhere—not exactly like this, but somehow—" Here I brought my sentence to an inane conclusion, shaking the Square about in a purposeless manner, much to the amusement of my Grandson, who burst out laughing louder than ever, and declared that I was not teaching him, but joking with him; and so saying he unlocked the door and ran out of the room. Thus ended my first attempt to convert a pupil to the Gospel of Three Dimensions.

22.—How I then tried to diffuse the Theory of Three Dimensions by other means, and of the result

My failure with my Grandson did not encourage me to communicate my secret to others of my household; yet neither was I led by it to despair of success. Only I saw that I must not wholly rely on the catch-phrase, "Upward, not Northward," but must rather endeavour to seek a demonstration by setting before the public a clear view of the whole subject; and for this purpose it seemed necessary to resort to writing.

So I devoted several months in privacy to the composition of a treatise on the mysteries of Three Dimensions. Only, with the view of evading the Law, if possible, I spoke not of a physical Dimension, but of a Thoughtland whence, in theory, a Figure could look down upon Flatland and see simultaneously the insides of all things, and where it was possible that there might be supposed to exist a Figure environed, as it were, with six Squares, and containing eight terminal Points. But in writing this book I found myself sadly hampered by the impossibility of drawing such diagrams as were necessary for my purpose; for of course, in our country of Flatland, there are no tablets but Lines, and no diagrams but Lines, all in one straight Line and only distinguishable by difference of size and brightness; so that, when I had finished my treatise (which I entitled,

"Through Flatland to Thoughtland") I could not feel certain that many would understand my meaning.

Meanwhile my life was under a cloud. All pleasures palled upon me; all sights tantalized and tempted me to outspoken treason, because I could not but compare what I saw in Two Dimensions with what it really was if seen in Three, and could hardly refrain from making my comparisons aloud. I neglected my clients and my own business to give myself to the contemplation of the mysteries which I had once beheld, yet which I could impart to no one, and found daily more difficult to reproduce even before my own mental vision.

One day, about eleven months after my return from Spaceland, I tried to see a Cube with my eye closed, but failed; and though I succeeded afterwards, I was not then quite certain (nor have I been ever afterward) that I had exactly realized the original. This made me more melancholy than before, and determined me to take some step; yet what, I knew not. I felt that I would have been willing to sacrifice my life for the Cause, if thereby I could have produced conviction. But if I could not convince my Grandson, how could I convince the highest and most developed Circles in the land?

And yet at times my spirit was too strong for me, and I gave vent to dangerous utterances. Already I was considered heterodox if not treasonable, and I was keenly alive to the danger of my position; nevertheless I could not at times refrain from bursting out into suspicious or half-seditious utterances, even among the highest Polygonal and Circular society. When, for example, the question arose about the treatment of those lunatics who said that they had received the power of seeing the insides of things, I would quote the saying of an ancient Circle, who declared that

prophets and inspired people are always considered
by the majority to be mad; and I could not help
occasionally dropping such expressions as "the eye
that discerns the interiors of things," and "the all-
seeing land"; once or twice I even let fall the forbidden terms "the Third and Fourth Dimensions." At
last, to complete a series of minor indiscretions, at a
meeting of our Local Speculative Society held at the
palace of the Prefect himself,—some extremely silly
person having read an elaborate paper exhibiting the
precise reasons why Providence has limited the number of Dimensions to Two, and why the attribute of
omnividence is assigned to the Supreme alone—I so
far forgot myself as to give an exact account of the
whole of my voyage with the Sphere into Space, and
to the Assembly Hall in our Metropolis, and then to
Space again, and of my return home, and of everything that I had seen and heard in fact or vision. At
first, indeed, I pretended that I was describing the
imaginary experiences of a fictitious person; but my
enthusiasm soon forced me to throw off all disguise,
and finally, in a fervent peroration, I exhorted all my
hearers to divest themselves of prejudice and to become believers in the Third Dimension.

Need I say that I was at once arrested and taken
before the Council?

Next morning, standing in the very place where
but a very few months ago the Sphere had stood in
my company, I was allowed to begin and to continue
my narration unquestioned and uninterrupted. But
from the first I foresaw my fate; for the President,
noting that a guard of the better sort of Policemen
was in attendance, of angularity little, if at all, under
55°, ordered them to be relieved before I began my
defence, by an inferior class of 2° or 3°. I knew only
too well what that meant. I was to be executed or

imprisoned, and my story was to be kept secret from the world by the simultaneous destruction of the officials who had heard it; and, this being the case, the President desired to substitute the cheaper for the more expensive victims.

After I had concluded my defence, the President, perhaps perceiving that some of the junior Circles had been moved by my evident earnestness, asked me two questions:—

1. Whether I could indicate the direction which I meant when I used the words "Upward, not Northward"?

2. Whether I could by any diagrams or descriptions (other than the enumeration of imaginary sides and angles) indicate the Figure I was pleased to call a Cube?

I declared that I could say nothing more, and that I must commit myself to the Truth, whose cause would surely prevail in the end.

The President replied that he quite concurred in my sentiment, and that I could not do better. I must be sentenced to perpetual imprisonment; but if the Truth intended that I should emerge from prison and evangelize the world, the Truth might be trusted to bring that result to pass. Meanwhile I should be subjected to no discomfort that was not necessary to preclude escape, and, unless I forfeited the privilege by misconduct, I should be occasionally permitted to see my brother who had preceded me to my prison.

Seven years have elapsed and I am still a prisoner, and—if I except the occasional visits of my brother—debarred from all companionship save that of my jailers. My brother is one of the best of Squares, just, sensible, cheerful, and not without fraternal affection; yet I confess that my weekly interviews, at least in one respect, cause me the bitterest pain. He was present when the Sphere manifested himself in the Council Chamber; he saw the Sphere's changing sections; he heard the explanation of the phenomena then given to the Circles. Since that time, scarcely a week has passed during seven whole years, without his hearing from me a repetition of the part I played in that manifestation, together with ample descriptions of all the phenomena in Spaceland, and the arguments for the existence of Solid things derivable from Analogy. Yet—I take shame to be forced to confess it—my brother has not yet grasped the nature of the Third Dimension, and frankly avows his disbelief in the existence of a Sphere.

Hence I am absolutely destitute of converts, and, for aught that I can see, the millennial Revelation has been made to me for nothing. Prometheus up in Spaceland was bound for bringing down fire for mortals, but I—poor Flatland Prometheus—lie here in prison for bringing down nothing to my countrymen. Yet I exist in the hope that these memoirs, in some manner, I know not how, may find their way to the minds of humanity in Some Dimension, and may stir up a race of rebels who shall refuse to be confined to limited Dimensionality.

That is the hope of my brightest moments. Alas, it is not always so. Heavily weighs on me at times the burdensome reflection that I cannot honestly say I am confident as to the exact shape of the once-seen, oft-regretted Cube; and in my nightly visions the mysterious precept, "Upward, not Northward," haunts me like a soul-devouring Sphinx. It is part of the martyrdom which I endure for the cause of the Truth that there are seasons of mental weakness, when Cubes and Spheres flit away into the background of scarce-possible existences; when the Land of Three Dimensions seems almost as visionary as the Land of

One or None; nay, when even this hard wall that bars me from my freedom, these very tablets on which I am writing, and all the substantial realities of Flatland itself, appear no better than the offspring of a diseased imagination, or the baseless fabric of a dream.